Whisper
Park Lane

by

Darren Swart

Whisper Park Lane

Cover Art by *Debbie Taylor*

The Wild Rose Press, Inc.
PO Box 708
Adams Basin, NY 14410-0708
Visit us at www.thewildrosepress.com

Publishing History
First Mainstream Mystery Edition, 2019
Print ISBN 978-1-5092-2625-2
Digital ISBN 978-1-5092-2626-9

Published in the United States of America

Dedication

For the 73 million Americans
who are struggling through life's circumstances.
My hope for the future is
for a better tomorrow for us all.

Chapter 1

Marge Hope walked Dalton over to the apartment next door. Miss Ruby had the door open waiting for them. Ruby sat in the cluttered living room with a plastic cup of orange soda beside her. An aging upright Kemble piano sat in the corner. Newspapers, magazines, dirty dishes, and old pizza boxes covered every surface of the room—everything except the Kemble. It was Miss Ruby's most prized possession. When Miss Ruby saw Marge, she smiled. Her eyes looked abnormally large through the thick lenses of her glasses. Miss Ruby cleared her throat. "Hey honey, do you think you could spot me a ten?"

Marge had twenty-five dollars to last until her next paycheck. It would be just enough to buy gas to get her back and forth to work and a loaf of bread for her and Dalton. She sighed, "Sure Ruby." She dug out a five and five ones and put the money in Ruby's hand. She couldn't say much; Ruby only charged her twenty-five a week to watch Dalton while she was at work, and Dalton could play the piano until nine. It was a good arrangement. Ruby taught piano her entire life, and Dalton loved playing piano. The old woman liked the boy's company and didn't charge, even though she coached him every night.

Marge hugged Dalton. "Be good for Miss Ruby, okay?"

Dalton looked up at his mom. "When have I ever been a problem?"

Marge gave him a faint smile and kissed him on the forehead. "You're right. How about, be helpful to Miss Ruby? Does that sound more like it?"

Dalton assured his mom, "I'll help her pick up the living room. How about that?"

Marge patted Dalton on the back. "That's more like it."

When Marge had left, Miss Ruby looked at Dalton. "Sweet boy, Miss Ruby needs to go to the alphabet store. Will you ride with me?"

Dalton had ridden with Miss Ruby to the liquor store just about every night he could remember. Every night it was the same conversation. Dalton nodded. "Yes, ma'am. I'll ride with you."

Ruby got up a little unsteadily, Dalton walked to her and steadied her. The old woman was almost the same height as Dalton, and he was only ten. She patted him on the arm letting him know she was okay and moved slowly to an armchair where her purse was nestled between a Fast 'N Fresh bag and a faded tapestry pillow. Ruby grabbed a burgundy shawl from the top of the chair and snuggled into the cover. She looked at Dalton. "Well, let's roll, partner." In what almost sounded like a Southwest drawl.

The wooden stairs creaked as the pair eased down one flight to the parking lot below. Ruby began to mutter to herself as she looked at the large four wheel drive truck parked beside her rusting minivan. She looked at Dalton and said, "Honey, you're going to have to let me pull out a bit because Rodriguez has parked his stinking truck too close to ol' Gertie again."

Ruby always named her vehicles. Ruby tossed her purse in the passenger seat and cranked the ancient minivan. After about three attempts, Gertie roared to life, further reinforcing that a new muffler was in order for the near future. Ruby eased the minivan forward so Dalton could get in the front seat beside her. The boy opened the door which groaned in protest because of dry hinges. Ruby reached across to throw her purse on the floor. As she did, her foot slipped from the brake. The minivan lurched forward throwing Dalton back, and the door slammed shut on the boy's hand. All Ruby could hear was Dalton scream.

****

The phone chirped on the bed stand. Cheryl pawed for it blindly and knocked a stack of precariously placed books to the floor. She gripped the phone and jabbed the key with her thumb. "Hello?"

The night nurse responded, "Hey, Cheryl, it's Louise. I hate to bother you, but we have a young patient with serious trauma to the right hand."

Cheryl covered her mouth as she yawned. "Can't Dr. Wise handle it?"

Louise replied, "Oh, he can handle it all right; he told the mother that it's best to amputate. His mama is asking for a second opinion."

Cheryl sat up in the bed and forced her eyes wide open. "How old is the patient?"

Louise responded, "He's ten; his mother said he's a very talented piano player."

Even being half-asleep, Cheryl could hear a woman wailing in the background. She took a deep breath to keep from saying what she was thinking; slowly and calmly she said, "I'll be there in fifteen.

3

Would you be a dear and keep Dr. Wise in a holding pattern?"

Louise replied, "I'll take care of him; be careful coming in. You just got off a double shift."

Cheryl responded, "Thanks, Louise."

Cheryl rolled her feet over the side of the bed to the coolness of the floor below. She could just make out the rumble of bass guitar at the party two doors down. Max grumbled at the interruption and opened one eye; he stretched and rolled over. She slid her hand over the silky tiger-striped fur along his back and was immediately rewarded with the sputtered purr reminiscent of an old Evinrude. He kneaded the cover and rolled into the warmth she left behind. She scowled. "You swine; try not to drool on the sheets."

The ugly yellow glare of the bedside lamp made him cover his face with a striped yellow paw. Cheryl stretched and shrugged off the numbness as she wandered to the bathroom. The toothpaste lay conveniently on the sink edge dripping into the basin, no lid to be found. An unopened make-up compact lay to the side buried under a toilet paper wrapper. She moved a hand towel to the side to find her toothbrush underneath. As she moved closer to the vanity, she stubbed her toe on a stack of dog-eared surgical technique books; colorful vellum markers gave the manuals festive colors despite their seriousness. For the hundredth time she made a mental promise to clean up the bathroom, along with the rest of her condo. She had been here two years now and unopened boxes acted as end tables for her worn couch. It didn't matter, Max didn't seem to care; besides, she spent most of her time at the hospital anyway. She wouldn't have it any other way.

She climbed into her old Alfa Romeo. A brisk wind foretelling an early North Carolina winter caught the door, and she struggled to close it.

Fifteen minutes later, Louise placed a cup of hot coffee in her hand. She sipped the fresh coffee. After twenty years as the night supervisor, Louise was feared by many, loved by most. The fear was well earned; she was a no-nonsense RN. Louise was built like a shot putter. Her powerful shoulders, short neck, and broad face made her look like she was ready to take the field.

Louise handed Cheryl the charts.

Cheryl scanned top down on the form. "Let's have a look, shall we?" She scowled at Dr. Wise's admission notes. "This is serious, but repairable. Why the rush to amputate?"

Louise looked at her over reading glasses. "Uninsured patient; we're almost out of beds."

Cheryl took a cleansing breath as she said, "Is the patient prepped?"

Louise removed her glasses. "Dr. Wise has him in pre-op; he's preparing for surgery himself."

Cheryl replied, "Fine, stall him long enough for me to talk to the mother."

Louise's pearly teeth lit her face. "I'll be happy to, Doctor."

She turned on her heel and walked like a drill sergeant to the OR. Cheryl sipped the strong black coffee as she reviewed Dr. Wise's notes and X-rays on her way to the waiting room. A frail woman clutched a threadbare blue sweater to her chest as she hovered at the window, staring at nothing in the blackness outside. Cheryl's voice was low. "Ms. Hope?" She jerked around, startled at the sound of Cheryl's voice. Her pale blue eyes looked drained; dark rings gathered under her eyes. Her bony fingers dragged frizzy strawberry split ends out of her eyes and tucked them behind her ear.

Cheryl extended a strong capable hand. "Ms. Hope, I'm Dr. Blumenthal. Everyone here calls me Cheryl."

The woman had an ice-cold grip that sent chills up Cheryl's spine, but there was quiet strength in it from such a fragile-looking woman. Strength born of desperation. Tears welled up in her eyes again. "It's my fault. If I had been there, none of this would have happened."

The admission made Cheryl pause, but she dodged the comment. "I am going to assist Dr. Wise in a second opinion in Dalton's case. It is a very complicated surgery; if we are successful, it could take him several months to recover from this."

Ms. Hope released her hand from her sweater and removed a tissue from her pocket. She dabbed her eyes, "Whatever it takes; if I have to wash windows and scrub toilets for the rest of my life, I'll do anything to pay for this. I work two jobs now, but I can squeeze in something somehow."

Cheryl focused on the task at hand to avoid the emotional wellspring. "Let's not worry about that right now. I think it would be best to focus on Dalton's recovery. When was the last time you slept?"

Ms. Hope blinked as if not comprehending the question. "I don't know, why?"

Cheryl replied, "Dalton will need you to be strong for him to get through this. He will be in surgery for several hours. I'm going to shut the door and let security know you are in here. You will be safe, so get some rest. I'll let you know when Dalton's out of surgery."

A degree of the angst left Ms. Hope's eyes. "So you'll come talk to me as soon as the surgery is done?"

Cheryl responded, "First thing; I promise. Would you like me to flip off the lights?"

Ms. Hope replied, "No, I don't like the dark; I can sleep with them on."

Cheryl replied, "Try not to worry."

Ms. Hope responded, "I'll try." She almost fell back on the couch.

Cheryl walked swiftly from the waiting room toward the OR. She met Willie, one of the night shift guards, as she hustled down the hall; she smiled at him. "Just the man I wanted to see. There's a Ms. Hope in the Surgery waiting room; I asked her to get some sleep. Could you check on her, get her a blanket and pillow, and maybe see if Andre has anything he can whip her up in the cafeteria?"

With a linebacker's build, he leaned over and returned the smile. "That's a tall order, Dr. B, but since it's you, I'll make sure it happens."

She kept walking and turned her head. "As always, my knight in shining armor."

A strong chocolate hand tipped the black ball cap. "Always."

****

Dr. Wise's brow furrowed deeply as she entered the room. It wasn't that he didn't respect her as a doctor; it was that he didn't *like* her. She always seemed to side with the patient, never considering that the hospital was a business. His tone was brusque. "Why are *you* here?"

Cheryl didn't blink. "The mother asked for a second opinion. I'm here to assist with that."

"I'm perfectly capable of handling this, thank you."

Cheryl narrowed her eyes. "Without a doubt, Doctor. But let's take a second look."

She stepped up to the X-rays. Wise didn't move. She moved next to him almost touching her shoulder to his arm. He glared down at her; she could see small patches of red forming in his widow's peak. Cheryl arched her eyebrows in response. His lips thinned as he stepped back. She studied the panel intensely for a moment; she could see the trauma quite clearly beginning at the pinky and radiating to the center finger. She methodically studied the patterns at the ligature points in the joints and surrounding the tendons. "I don't understand why we need to amputate; I do need another series of X-rays here and here." She pointed to anterior portions of the finger. "These are worthless. Who took these?"

Dr. Wise replied, "Don did. Why?"

Cheryl pointed at the film. "They're not what we need. Have him run another series; I want to see this before we go in. Is the team assembled?"

Dr. Wise replied, "Yes." His voice almost hissed as he said it.

Cheryl looked up. "Good. Are you available to assist?"

Dr. Wise's eyes were slits now. "Since when did you become the chief surgeon?"

Cheryl replied calmly, "Since I specialized in plastic and reconstructive surgery at Riverside. It's why you hired me, remember?"

Dr. Wise responded, "Well, it doesn't sound like

you need me to assist, then. The patient is your responsibility now; it will most likely end up in a malpractice lawsuit judging by the looks of the mother. Look, Cheryl, the world doesn't care about the individual—it only cares about the majority."

Cheryl furrowed her brow. "Maybe it's time for us to care about the individual, Doctor."

****

Her team performed flawlessly during the hours it took to repair the hair-like veins, muscles, bones, and nerves in Dalton's fingers. The post-op orders put him in the burn ward to reduce the risk of infection. Louise made it clear that if the boy contracted a staph infection on her shift, every nurse would be drawn and quartered, regardless of who was at fault. The entire ward smelled like a bleach factory. Louise paraded the halls like a warden after lockdown. So long as their young ward was under the scrutiny of Louise the Hun, he would be fine until she could check back with him.

Cheryl plopped back on the bench in post-op; she reached up, pulled the surgical cap from her head, feeling her hair plastered to her scalp by sweat. Fatigue rolled across her like breakers at the beach; she closed her eyes just for a moment. When she snorted fifteen minutes later, it was loud enough that she woke with a start. Embarrassed, she looked around; she was the only one in the room. She hauled herself up from the bench and left post-op. She met Willie at the nurse's station nervously fidgeting with his radio. Cheryl powered through the numbness. "How's Ms. Hope?"

Willie dropped his head. "I'm sorry, Dr. B; she left."

Cheryl glared. "How could we just let her go like

9

that?"

Louise looked up. "Honey, this is a hospital, not a prison."

Cheryl responded, "But he doesn't have anyone here."

Louise came around the corner of the counter and placed her hand on Cheryl's shoulder. "She said she would lose her job. The boy will have to leave here some day; it would be nice if he didn't have to move into a cardboard box when that day comes."

Cheryl snorted. "She could find another job."

Louise replied, "Maybe if you are one of the best doctors in the country, but not if you're a convenience store clerk earning minimum wage and there are four other people trying to take your job."

Cheryl rubbed the back of her neck. "I'm sorry; you're right. I need to see his chart."

Louise placed a gentle hand on her back. "Sweetie, why don't you go home and get some sleep? I'd say you've done enough for one night. I'll make sure they call you if there is a problem."

Cheryl replied, "I will, but there is one more thing I need to do."

****

The sun peeped over the horizon casting a crimson glow on the lone sugar maple in front of the hospital. The air was brisk as she walked out the main lobby doors toward her car. She snuggled deeper into her jacket as she braced against the chilled air. The leather seats of the Alfa Romeo felt cold even through the fabric of the scrubs. She coaxed the old car to life as it sputtered and complained about being asked to perform so early. Her mechanic warned her it would always be a "bit cold-natured." He was right. She looked across the faded hood thinking once again she really needed to get a new paint job. That was hard to do when you took patients pro bono, like her mechanic's son. She had corrected his cleft lip; in exchange he provided her with free labor on her car. She still had to pay for the parts.

Ms. Hope had listed her contact location as *Night Shift Clerk—Fast and Fresh Food Store.* There was nothing fresh in the neighborhood where it was located. The streets were deserted in the early morning hours except for an occasional underweight dog. Still, as she pulled into the parking lot, she locked her car under the neon glare. Cheryl hurried past the barred storefront windows and wondered how anyone could work in a place like this. She looked down as her foot clinked against an empty crack vial on the sidewalk; she almost jumped in response. She walked toward the front doors and looked down at a lump beside the door.

The lump looked up with bleary eyes and asked, "Hey lady, you gotta smoke?"

Cheryl replied, "No, I'm sorry, I don't smoke."

The lump dropped his head once again. She couldn't explain why she had apologized to the man for not smoking when she admonished her patients for it. Inside, Ms. Hope stood behind the counter trying to keep warm in the frigid store. It almost felt colder inside the store than it did outside. The smell of cigar smoke reached her; it almost made her ill. Cheryl looked away from Ms. Hope to see a greasy man smashing bread onto the shelf; even in the coolness of the store, she could see the sweat glistening on his forehead. He glared back at her but kept stuffing. Cheryl reached out and touched Ms. Hope's hand gently. "Hello, Ms. Hope."

Ms. Hope looked at her with watery eyes. "Please call me Marge."

Cheryl began again, maintaining her composure. "Thank you, Marge. I just wanted to let you know the surgery went very well. Dalton will be in the burn ward for about five to seven days—"

The large man with thick greasy hair standing in the bread aisle spoke loudly, "Lady, you botherin' my clerk?"

Marge looked at him. "It's okay, Big Mike. She's a doctor; she operated on my boy last night."

"Is she gonna pay your damn bills when you ain't workin' no more? You got things to do, woman; stop your yappin' and get to work!"

Cheryl whirled around. "Her son was in an accident and almost lost his hand; I was trying to tell her he's going to be okay!" She felt the heat rise on the back of her neck.

Big Mike rolled his cigar from one side of his mouth to the other and continued to mangle bread into the shelves. "Yeah, well, I got a store to keep afloat here; we've all got problems, ain't we? Buy something or leave."

Cheryl snatched up a pack of gum and slammed it on the counter. "As I said, Dalton will be in the burn ward to reduce the risk of infection. It will be several days before we will know if the surgery was successful enough to save his fingers."

She dropped a wrinkled dollar on the counter. As Marge reached for it, she tenderly touched the back of her hand. "Please see me when you can; we'll work with the hospital social worker to get you some assistance with his care."

Marge looked like she wanted to cry again but didn't. Her voice was so low Cheryl could barely hear her. "Thanks for shopping at Fast and Fresh, please come again."

Cheryl shot Big Mike a dirty look as he stuffed bread onto the shelves. He didn't look up as she left.

Chapter 2

The engine hummed smoothly down the long stretch of back road. The sun warmed the autumn air making it the perfect combination of warmth laced with crispness. The top was neatly tucked back allowing her to feel the warm sun on her face while giving her an unobstructed view of the luscious foliage of orange and red which dotted the pastures. The back road was all but forgotten by the locals.

The only storm clouds were the ones Cheryl could feel in her eyes. She drew her lips thin and tight as she squinted at the road ahead as if trying to find something that wasn't there. The conversation kept rolling through her mind like a tape recorder. She played it over and over in her head:

Ray's plastic facial expression was only outdone by his plastic hair. Cheryl wondered if he had stock in hair gel production. "Dr. Blumenthal, when you have time, could you swing by my office so we can have a chat?"

Cheryl replied, "I'm free now, Ray."

Ray smiled with his mouth. "Excellent, let's go to my office."

As he walked ahead of her, the sound of his polyester pants swishing together reminded her of the sound of a swinging axe. As she entered his office, three things struck her: the plushness of his new carpeting; the freshly stocked salt-water aquarium; and the sickening sweet smell of Dr. Wise's cologne.

Ray's whitened teeth resembled more of a snarl than a smile as he motioned her to sit next to Dr. Wise.

Cheryl responded politely, "I'll stand, thank you."

Ray pulled out an orange file and flipped it open. She recognized the top page of the file, the one with her signature emblazoned across the bottom; after she had signed it, she had carried Ray's one hundred dollar zebrawood pen to the aquarium and dropped it in. The page still bore the ripples of salt water where he had frantically tried to salvage the pen before the seated ink cartridge split from swelled wood fibers. Yeah, that page. She was rarely impulsive; it seemed that impulsive moments came back to haunt her.

Ray began quite professionally, "As we have discussed on previous occasions, it is Wise Regional Medical Center's policy to give the best care available to the patient. Doctors are encouraged to make the best decision when it comes to caring for the patient. We all applaud your efforts to reduce suffering and go the extra mile, but..."

Cheryl thought to herself, *Yeah, there always seemed to be a "but."*

"...we must manage our costs or we will not be able to compete with County General. So, I am formally putting you on administrative leave pending a formal board hearing."

Cheryl asked, "So you're giving me the week off?"

Ray looked a little surprised. "Technically, it is not viewed as a vacation, merely a cooling off period for the staff to understand the facts surrounding this case."

Cheryl pushed a bit. "With or without pay?"

He blinked. "Well, with pay, I suppose."

Dr. Wise glared at Ray. Cheryl couldn't believe the absurdity of it all. She asked, "Who will be managing my patients?"

Ray replied, "Why, Dr. Wise, of course."

Dr. Wise's lips formed a V. He looked like a comic book villain. She knew if there was any sign of infection in Dalton's hand, he would put the boy back under the knife and amputate, just to spite her.

Cheryl replied, "I'm sure this would add an unfairness to Dr. Wise's case load. May I make a suggestion?"

Ray's expression was emotionless. "I'm sorry; this is not a negotiation, Dr. Blumenthal. Dr. Wise is fully capable of integrating your patients into his rounds until this is sorted out."

She arched her eyebrow and gave him a droll look. "You're too kind."

Ray reached for his new Nigerian pearwood pen in his shirt pocket and thought better of it. Instead, he reached into his desk drawer and pulled out a disposable Bic pen instead.

****

A sudden gust of wind sent a flurry of leaves into the car. Cheryl batted them out of the way as she drove on. For the first time since she left the hospital, she looked around her. Even though she didn't know exactly where she was, everything looked familiar somehow. A leaning street sign ahead made her slow down. She could just make out the faded letters on an antique wooden street sign *Whisper Park Lane*. A chill went down her spine. She eased the Alfa onto the side road, which went from paved to dirt in a matter of feet.

Even though not well maintained, the matted dirt and grass formed firm ground from heavy use.

She eased the car down the road to avoid wrecking her undercarriage from the large rocks laid down for heavy equipment. Gradually the white oaks and hickory trees turned to loblolly pines. The gentle rustle of leaves transformed to the whisper of the wind through the stand of evergreens. For the first time in days, she smiled. It smelled like home; maybe because it *was* home.

She cringed as the undergrowth crunched beneath the car as she pulled into the driveway. She stopped before driving very far and killed the engine. The house didn't look the same. The boarded windows and faded paint looked foreign compared to when she had last been here. It seemed like a century had passed. The porch was smaller than she remembered. But then everything tends to seem larger when you are a child. Still it was built how porches used to be, long and rambling like the house itself. She tested the first step with the ball of her foot before climbing the stairs to the top. The boards were as solid as the day she left the house, a testament to her father's carpentry skills, but not his character. She eased up the steps slowly disturbing only dust as she moved.

As she reached the top step, she noted the rather official looking posting stapled to the front door. She straightened the folded corner out on the notice, which read:

This Structure is Condemned
By Order of the Department of Transportation
Pursuant to the construction of the future I-61 Corridor...

She shook her head in dismay. She walked around the corner of the L-shaped porch and found an old rocker moving in the breeze. She brushed the leaves from the rocker and plopped heavily into the seat. This had been the porch she'd read Ian Fleming and Truman Capote on long rainy summer days; the porch she contemplated life on as she became a teenager; and the porch she had studied on in high school. She sat now considering her precarious position at the hospital. She sat in the stillness of the day trying to turn off the anxiety that churned within her. The pines swayed in an undulating dance. The soft whisper of the trees began to bring back memories. She had not thought about this place in years; in fact, she had shut out the memory of this place to bottle up the bad—at the cost of shutting out the good as well. There were so many memories about this place, her parents, Granny Ruth, her awkward teenage years.

The memory of her father going out for bread one night and the long, lonely wait for him to return. She had almost forgotten the feel of her mother's touch the next morning, as she combed through her hair while she slept on the couch. She clearly remembered the wellspring of anger she unleashed on her mother for not holding him there somehow. In the end, they both realized he wasn't coming back. Cheryl watched as the life drained from her mother's eyes as the realization hit them both. Her mother shut down, disappearing into the bedroom. She heard the weeping, interchanged with the occasional sob. It went on for days. Her mother emerged from the bedroom days later, hair matted, eyes red and vacant. Cheryl had flown into a frenzy of cleaning so that when her mother emerged the house would be clean. Her mother walked straight past the shine of lemon polish to the front door and stared at the yard below. The scattered pieces of her husband's prized tackle box spread across the yard where Cheryl had thrown it in anger. Lures and bobbers littered the yard.

All her mother said was, "You had better pick up all that fishing stuff before someone steps on it." Nothing else. There was no "Don't worry, we'll be fine," or "We're better off without him." Not a single word of hope. Her mother never healed from it; in some respects, neither had Cheryl. Cheryl shunned relationships, bottled up her frustrations without a word, worked frantically trying to keep everything running, without asking for help.

It had been Granny Ruth who helped Cheryl find her way out of the fog in those days. Granny Ruth was one of the few people she could still look in the eye without fear of judgement. She relived the moment when the little old woman's rotund backside swished as she waddled by. She had a different flowered housecoat for every day of the week. It was a while before Cheryl realized it was the only thing she ever wore. Granny Ruth volunteered to take care of her while her mother worked the night shift; it paid better, helping them with keeping an income flowing until they could find a smaller place. Granny Ruth had watched her for nothing.

Cheryl remembered sitting in Granny Ruth's kitchen on an old orange crate listening to the sizzle of pot roast in the well-seasoned broiler pan, and smelling the divineness of the green beans and potatoes slowly cooking on the gas burner. She almost laughed out loud remembering the Granny Ruth grunt as she rolled out the dough on the old white enamel table. There were no measuring spoons or cups as she dabbed a little of this, dolloped a bit of that. She rolled the pie dough with the vigor and speed of an expert. As she slapped the dough into the pie pan, her meaty hands removed the excess dough with a butter knife. Cheryl watched in fascination as she slung the pie pan into the oven with utter disregard to subtlety. When the pie shell was ready, she whipped the lemon, cream, egg yolks, and sugar together.

The old woman's eyes twinkled as she asked Cheryl, "So dear, what are you going to be when you grow up?"

Cheryl looked up in thought. "I dunno. Maybe a doctor, I guess."

Granny Ruth grunted as she pushed herself up from the table. From around her neck she removed a small silver angel and leaned across, placing it on the girl's neck. "There you go, an Angel of Mercy for an Angel of Mercy. That will carry you a long way; it has carried me."

Cheryl touched the small figure carefully. She was filled with wonder at the simple gesture. She looked up at the old woman. "I don't have anything to return the favor."

Ruth replied, "You just make it through medical school; that will be return enough for me." With that, she began to roll out biscuit dough on the counter.

It was a milestone moment of sorts for Cheryl. Her teachers saw a different child before them. Her drive was unstoppable; the faculty was challenged to keep up with her. Eleven years later she sat fiddling impatiently with the heavy cum laude medal and wondering when the ceremony would be over; no one in the audience waited for her as she left the stage. She was alone, and that was fine with her. Thinking back on that moment, it was only now sitting on this decrepit porch that she realized the seed Granny Ruth planted in her had come full circle to this place. Frustration sowed a different seed now; one that carried the burden that she had never been able to acknowledge the simple gift of an old woman who died in her second year of med school.

Her eyes drifted across the peeling porch rail, across the untamed clumps of yellow straw grass to the unstoppable grove of evergreens below the house. Brightly hued clouds glowed with the fiery orange sunbeams into the green of loblollies. The trees scraped mindlessly against the rusting metal of the singlewide mobile home abandoned and almost invisible in the grove. Cheryl's jaw tightened at the sound of it; the decay of the place she once called home reopened long-forgotten wounds.

The vibrancy of what this place had once been seemed alien to her now. All she could think of was that the principles born in this place had launched her beyond the mediocrity of her peers; it drove her to be more to her patients than a healer. She wanted to fix the pain in their souls. Now, small-minded administrators worried with budgets wanted her gone. *Her,* of all people; the one doctor in the hospital that patients didn't mind seeing, even if it was bad news. Her patients always knew she would fight with them side by side to the end.

Her throat tightened; she took a ragged breath in defiance of the unyielding tears that forced their way forward. Despite her bottomless will, she could not keep them away. Tracks streamed down her cheeks as she dropped her head in defeat. She wept at the absurdity of it all, she wept at the fear of not being able to go back, and she wept at the thought that she had lost this place from her life. The bitterness of the moment was exacerbated by realization that she was alone. She had no close friends other than the hospital. The only true lover she ever had drifted away after med school. She had not spoken to Amit in over a year. She could not reach out to him now in desperation; that would seem pathetic.

Amidst the melancholy, a quiet sad melody ebbed forth in her mind. The strokes of piano called to her, as if they were a plea from the center of her being. She could hear the notes in her head as clearly as if the ivory were in front of her. Granny Ruth had played it for her on the ancient Philco record player. Chopin's "Raindrops" drifted through her. Note after note welled forth, pushing away the pain. She felt a sudden calm within her, a calm that buoyed her, made her believe it would all be okay. She focused on the rusting steel shell of the singlewide. She envisioned Granny Ruth smiling as she washed dishes in the kitchen window below, despite the pine limb which poked its way out of the hole where a window once was. She wiped the tears with the back of her hand and hoped against hope that it would all turn out okay.

In the yard below, a tall figure weaved quietly through the swaying sprigs of broom straw and around the fallen gutter onto the porch. His dark hair was dotted in silver at the temples making him almost distinguished despite his slump. Nothing would hide his square hawkish nose and piercing hazel eyes; it made him appear cruel and hard. A well-oiled shotgun rested in his hands and glinted in the hues of the afternoon sun. Quietly he eased behind Cheryl.

Chapter 3

The creak of a floorboard wrenched Cheryl out of her reverie. She blinked away the tears and held her breath, listening closely.

A voice sounded behind her. "Ma'am? Are you all right?"

Cheryl wiped away the tears hurriedly. Her jaw clinched as she took a deep breath to clear her head. She stood and faced her mystery man. Her eyes were still red as she looked up. His expressionless eyes contradicted the question. None of this mattered once her eyes rested on the glint of the large gun held loosely in the man's hands. She wasn't sure if she needed to vault the porch rail and run or talk her way out of this. She chose the latter.

Sheepishly she looked at her feet. "I'm sorry to intrude. It was so peaceful here...and I needed to think."

A tiny half smile turned one corner of his mouth upward. "It ain't exactly on the tourist maps, but it sure is quiet here. Sorry about the shotgun—I've had to run off kids trying to cook up that meth mess. Sure is a tragedy. That and this is a pretty dangerous place, ma'am."

She almost stopped breathing. "Dangerous?"

"Yes, ma'am. The road crews are slated to tear this place down. I'm surprised they're not here today." He rolled his eyes upward thoughtfully. "And then again, maybe I'm not." He chuckled at his own joke.

She raised her eyebrows, but her eyes remained fixed on the shotgun. The old man noticed her look. He set the weapon carefully to the side. "Sorry, ma'am. Dove season is in, so I was trying to see if I could muster up a little supper. I don't mean to be forward, but it seems a bit off the beaten track for anyone to show up here."

She nudged a leaf with the toe of her shoe. "I used to live here a long time ago. I was out driving and just ended up here."

He nodded understandingly. "A lot of people have ended up in Whisper Park Lane that way. If you don't mind my asking, when did you live here?"

Almost dismissively she said, "It seems like a lifetime. I guess it's been over twenty years."

His next question surprised her. "Who was your mother?"

Her brow furrowed as she looked up into his almost silvery eyes; she tried to decide if she trusted him. He had a deeply soulful look in his eyes that convinced her. Hesitantly she replied, "Camille, Camille Blumenthal. Why do you ask?"

He grinned and raised his hand for a shake. "So, you must be Cher, and all grown up at that."

She couldn't hide her surprise as she shook his hand. No one had called her by her nickname since she was a girl. "How do you know that name?"

"Anyone who knew Granny Ruth knew you."

She felt a lump rise in her throat. She wanted to cry again and got mad at herself for going all to hell inside. The old man extended an open palm toward her. "The name's Horace. Horace Peebles, it's a pleasure to meet you, Dr. Blumenthal."

His grip was strong and sure. As was Cheryl's. She almost stammered when she responded, "It's nice to meet you, Horace."

"It's an honor, really, ma'am. I know you're a doctor and all, but if you have time, feel free to swing by my place and we'll have tea."

She blinked. "I'm sorry?"

Horace replied, "Just trying to be social, ma'am. I meant nothing by it."

Cheryl relaxed. "I'll try to make it by in the next couple of days."

He shoved his hand into his pocket and removed a folded envelope with writing on both sides; he found a small space and jotted his address and phone in a steady hand; he carefully tore the strip from the envelope and handed it to her. "Call me if you need directions."

She took the piece of paper. "I will."

He gave her an awkward sideways grin. "I hope to see you soon, Doctor."

Cheryl replied, "Likewise, Horace, and call me Cheryl."

*****

She muttered as she scrounged through unopened boxes. She sneezed without warning and scared Max into the other room. At the bottom of the pile she unearthed a tattered box from her childhood. As she filtered through the contents, memories were attached to the odd assortment of pieces; some memories were good, some were not. In a small box by itself, she found what she was looking for—a small sterling angel. It was smaller than she remembered. She put it on and fingered the fine filigree. The phone broke the silence. It seemed unnecessarily loud, making the cat jump again and grumble at the interruption.

She picked it up just to stop the noise. "Yes?"

Louise responded, "Honey, it's Louise. I have a slight problem; could you give me some advice?"

Cheryl stopped fingering the angel. "Of course."

Louise continued, "I have a patient here in the ER who said he was burned. He doesn't have any burns, but he is at risk for infection. Do you follow?"

Cheryl replied, "Clearly, go on."

Louise responded, "I have a doctor who is recommending that we move the patient to a regular room to free up the expense of the patient staying in a room that requires intensive care. Is there a possibility that infection could set in, if the patient is moved to a regular ward with a roommate?"

Cheryl replied, "Have the patient's, uh, wounds covered over and is the tissue warm?"

Louise responded, "The surgery scars have closed; the cutaneous tissue diffusion appears normal and responsive to painful stimuli."

Cheryl replied, "That sounds promising. The patient might benefit from a hyperbaric oxygen treatment to the affected area outside of the unit."

Louise responded, "That can be arranged. Thank you, Doctor."

Cheryl laid the phone down. She knew the next call Louise made would be to Dr. Carroll, one of Cheryl's night shift pals. Dr. Carroll, known as Boomer from his college football days, would write the order. Dr. Wise would initial it, only because Boomer and Wise shared the same alma mater. Louise kept her updated daily. It irked Cheryl that Dr. Wise had not bothered to look at the boy in two days, and yet he was quick to write the order to have him moved. She sat back and chewed her lip. In two days, there would be a hearing. They would decide her fate with the hospital. While moving to another practice did not concern her, the thoughts of leaving her patients did. She had fought so hard to be a good doctor, she didn't even want to consider leaving her patients behind—especially Dalton.

The thought of the boy all alone made her cringe. If she couldn't see him as a doctor, she could as a friend. She reached out and gave Max a scratch. She could feel him purr in response. She grabbed a gray hoodie and headed for the door. Halfway across the room, the phone chimed again. Irritated she moved back. "Hello?"

The voice asked, "Dr. Blumenthal?"

Cheryl replied, "Yes? Can I help you?" The voice sounded familiar.

The voice continued, "Yes ma'am, we met the other day at the Whisper Park Lane property. My name is Horace Peebles."

Cheryl replied, "Yes, Mr. Peebles, I recall meeting you the other day."

Horace responded, "Well, ma'am, I got to thinkin', I've got the old box of stuff from Ruth's. Would you like it?"

Cheryl replied, "I don't know what to say, Mr. Peebles."

Horace responded, "It's Horace, ma'am, and I'm pretty sure Ruth would have wanted you to have it."

Cheryl asked, "Why is that, Horace?"

Horace responded, "Well, because she wrote

'Cher' on the side of it." Cheryl was quiet for a moment. Horace broke the silence. "Ma'am, are you still there?"

Cheryl replied, "I'm here, Horace. I'm just a little surprised, is all."

Horace responded, "That's all right, ma'am. Ruth did that with all of us."

Cheryl asked, "Is tomorrow okay?"

Horace replied, "Sure; come around two."

Cheryl responded, "I'll be there."

Cheryl stared at the phone as she hung up. She couldn't imagine what the old woman would have left her. She tried not to dwell on it before going to the door.

Chapter 4

The early morning sun was streaming into the hospital as she stood at the threshold of the lobby. She took a deep breath before entering the lobby. This was the first time she had ever entered the hospital as anything other than an acting physician. It was still difficult for her to comprehend how she could be on suspension for acting compassionately. She caught a glimpse of Louise in the hall. Her starched white uniform stood out dramatically against the deep chocolate of her skin. It was old school compared to the cartoon characters on the scrubs of her subordinates. Louise didn't care. She looked over her reading glasses at Cheryl as she walked up. The young doctor was acutely aware she looked completely out of character in gray sweatpants and a ratty hoodie; she wore a faded red fishing cap. "Honey, you know you're not supposed to be here."

"As a doctor, yes, but as a visitor, I can come see my friends."

Louise was direct in her response. "I would keep old home week to a minimum if I were you."

Cheryl replied, "I'll be good, I promise. What room is Dalton in?" Louise arched her eyebrow and looked down at the chart in her hand. Cheryl raised her hand in an oath. "Just as a visitor, I promise."

Louise looked at her sternly. "If I see you so much

as put a Band-Aid on that boy, I will bounce you myself."

Cheryl grinned and replied, "Understood."

Louise moved forward like a small tank without saying another word. Two floors down, she led Cheryl into a double room with a single occupant. Louise looked at . "It's the best I could do with such short notice."

Cheryl replied, "It's fine." She eased into the room. She met the watery blue gaze of Marge Hope. Her face was drawn and tired, but she had a little more color to her skin.

Cheryl patted her arm gently. "I thought you might like some company."

Dalton's warm brown eyes and cherub smile lit the room. "Hey, Dr. Cheryl, they moved me out of that other room. This one has a lot more room!"

She flashed a broad smile at him. "It looks like we can set you up with your own piano in here."

Dalton replied, "Yep. I sure will be glad when I can play again."

Cheryl responded, "Me too. Say, buddy, would you like something cold to drink?"

Dalton grinned. "Boy, would I."

Cheryl replied, "Okay, you stay put, and we'll be right back."

Marge looked up as Cheryl placed a hand on her back. "I'm going to buy your mom a cup of coffee and we'll get you a cold drink."

Dalton responded, "Wow! That's great. Could you make it an orange soda?"

Cheryl replied, "Sure!"

Marge hesitantly rose from the chair, looking at

Dalton as she straightened up. He gave his mom a reassuring look. "It's okay, Mom. I'll be fine."

The odd exchange struck Cheryl, but she didn't question it. It almost appeared that Dalton was providing emotional support for his mom, not the other way around. She tucked her arm neatly around Marge's and asked, "So, do you like cafeteria coffee?"

****

The elevator chimed as they reached their arrival to the ground floor. Marge opened her mouth to speak and closed it. Her eyes were almost pleading; for what Cheryl had no idea. When Marge finally got the nerve up to speak, her voice was so low Cheryl could hardly hear her. "They said you got in trouble for helping my boy."

Cheryl put her hand on the frail shoulder. "I need you to understand Dalton's surgery is not the reason for any problems I'm having."

Marge tried to keep from breaking down. "But that one hateful doctor said you had been suspended and he had taken over my boy's care. He made it sound like you made a mistake."

Cheryl took a deep breath in and let it out slowly. She could feel her temper starting to flare. She focused on Marge. "He didn't mean there was a problem with the surgery. What he meant was I didn't follow the hospital procedure in cases like your son's." She was careful not to mention anything about insurance. "He was correct in that I didn't follow hospital policy to a tee."

Marge looked at her quizzically. "Is that why you're here now?"

Cheryl returned her look earnestly. "I'm here

because I wanted to visit with you and Dalton."

The older woman shook her head. "Why do you care? He's just another patient."

The retort stung, but Cheryl didn't let it deter her. She rubbed the tiny angel around her neck. "No, Marge, I'm a doctor because a long time ago, there was a person who helped me understand that being a doctor was something you had to believe in, not because it's a paycheck. I'm here because I care about you and Dalton."

Marge looked down. "You're the only one."

"What do you mean?"

"I told my boss at the furniture factory that I needed to spend more time with my boy. He told me that was fine, I could spend as much time as I wanted to, and then he fired me." She shook her head. "I've still got my nighttime job at the Fast and Fresh."

Cheryl tried to remain upbeat. "We'll figure something out. Let's help Dalton with his recovery, okay?"

Marge looked like she was going to cry again. She said nothing, but only nodded. The dark frothy liquid rose aromatically from the white Styrofoam cup as she poured the fresh coffee from a stainless steel pot. The women sat at the closest table. Marge cupped the stark white cup with both hands trying to absorb the heat. When she began to speak it was if someone had opened a floodgate. "He's such a sweet boy. I've done everything I can to keep him safe from problems, but I'm running out of time. His daddy walked out one night for cigarettes and never came back. It was probably for the best, but I can't seem to keep it all together for him." A teardrop dotted the table in front of her.

Cheryl placed her hand ever so gently on the older woman's. "My father left when I was twelve. My mother did the best she could, but she never got over it. This is not your fault."

Marge looked up. She looked at Cheryl with new eyes. She wiped her eyes and used a napkin to blow her nose. As she looked into Cheryl's eyes, empathy was all Cheryl could see. "Honey, I'm so sorry. I know this must be opening old wounds for you. I didn't know."

Cheryl shook her head sadly. "There's no way you could know. I grew past it. So will Dalton. But *we* need to figure out how to get him through this."

Marge looked up. Her attention was drawn to a figure behind Cheryl. Her expression changed. A chill went down Cheryl's spine at the sound of a familiar voice to her back. She began to rub the angel furiously trying to see if she could disappear.

Dr. Wise looked over the figure in the gray warm-up suit at Ms. Hope. "Ms. Hope, isn't it?"

Marge regarded him cautiously. "Yes, Doctor. How are you today?"

He flashed a big toothy grin. "Grand, thank you. Hope you have a nice day." He walked away whistling a happy tune to himself.

Marge looked at Cheryl dourly. "Do you think he even knows they moved him?"

Cheryl let out a silent sigh of relief. "I doubt it. Let's get back up to see Dalton."

Marge and Cheryl stood to leave.

Chapter 5

The Alfa Romeo idled down the twelve-foot tunnel of immaculately trimmed Nellie Stevens hollies. The crunch of fresh gravel beneath the tires added unique dimension to the corridor. As she exited the hollies, she faced the dramatic two-story farmhouse before her. She sat for a moment trying to determine where the front door was amidst the hedges along the enormous porch, dwarfed by the house behind it. The white clapboards gleamed against the coal blackness of hinged shutters. Even in the onslaught of fall the grass was healthy and green against splashes of gold and crimson from sugar maples in the forest behind the home. For a home that was so beautiful, it bore the impression of sterility. It was magazine perfect, with all the manicured shrubs, perfectly trimmed grass, and not a stone out of place.

Horace came out of the house and onto the front porch, smiling broadly. "Come on in, Cher. Glad you could make it."

She responded with a reserved smile. "Thank you, Horace. You have a beautiful home."

Horace replied, "It's the old home place. When I die, the kids will probably put it on the auction block. Neither of them wants anything to do with it, or me."

She winced mentally at the hint of discord. "I'm sorry to hear that."

He gave her a wry look. "Not to worry; things

change." He changed the subject. "Could I interest you in a cup of tea?"

Cheryl responded, "Red Rose if you have any."

Horace's eyes sparkled. "Absolutely."

She climbed the broad steps to the sturdy round columns framing the entrance to the porch. She felt like a child against the massiveness of the home. He held the door as she entered the house. She squinted in the dimness of the hall which was the polar opposite of the outside. Browns and umbers absorbed all of the light from the outside; the main living room was another story, however. The room popped with richness, in both texture and belongingness. She could envision generations gathered around a ten-foot Christmas tree singing and laughing. The ceiling seemed to touch the sky, dressed in elegant lines of formed tin culminating in a small chandelier in the center of the room. Age had tempered the half-paneled knotty pine to a golden hue leaving the room comfortable and warm. The eclectic array of furniture mixed comfortable overstuffed leather couches and austere wing-back chairs. A massive stone fireplace snapped and crackled merrily filling the room with warmth. Pictures of family filled every end table and every nook; a tall gilt-edged frame showcased a handsome couple which caught her eye. It wasn't difficult for her to recognize the rather hawkish nose of the man. "You made a lovely couple."

He shook his head sadly. "Ester was the glue that held this family together. We were married for forty years before cancer took her." He looked at Cheryl thoughtfully. "You know Ruth and Ester were sisters."

Cheryl shook her head as she made the connection between Horace and Ruth. "No, I didn't know that.

Were you close?"

Horace replied, "Yeah, I was closer to Ruth than I was to my own sisters. She was a sweet old bird. I guess that's why I let her stay on after Ester died. I miss 'em both."

Cheryl nodded silently.

Horace continued, "Well, why don't you have a seat, and I'll fetch the tea."

Cheryl responded, "That would be lovely."

As she sat a large golden retriever padded quietly into the room and sauntered over to Cheryl and leaned against her leg as she sat on the couch. His tail wagged furiously as he stood before her. She leaned forward, scratched him on the head, and moved down his back. His entire rear began to wag as he tried to lick her. She giggled, which only spurred him on.

Horace walked back into the room. "Barley! Leave that poor woman alone."

Barley paid his master no heed. Cheryl scratched his back affectionately. "He's fine, really."

Horace responded, "He'll worry you to death, ma'am. How do you like your tea?"

Cheryl answered, "Cream and sugar will be fine."

Horace spoke to Barley, "Come on, meathead." Barley broke away from Cheryl and followed his master to the front door. Horace opened the door and let the dog out. "Tea will be right up, ma'am."

Cheryl meandered through the room, settling on the soft gleam of old leather-bound books on either side of the fireplace. She browsed through the titles, settling on one, *The Whisper* by Mae Peebles. Carefully she removed it from the shelf and opened it gently, careful not to damage the old pages. The first poem was entitled "Park Lane." The title intrigued her; the poem startled her.

I see his hair in the copper of commerce,
I see his eyes dance in the waters of blue,
I see his countenance in the majesty of the Ash,
And the solemn wind sings of my love across the
morning dew,
Park Lane,
Park Lane.

~

He has traveled far to keep us safe from
aggression,
My heart yearns for word of his fate,
And yet it is I, who suffers from their oppression,
No letters come, alone I must wait

~

In the flurry of flight,
Winds push wings to air,
Mourning Doves sing of my plight,
Is this more than I can bear?
Park Lane,
Park Lane.

~

Men return each day,
Some covered in brown,
Some covered in gray,
I see him in all,
I see him in none,

~

And the gentle pines whisper,
Park Lane,
Park Lane…

Horace carried in a tea tray and set it on the end

table by the couch. "My grandmother wrote that. She was pretty good from what they say."

"It's beautiful. It mentions Park Lane—was that a real person?"

Horace replied, "The story goes, Grandmother was engaged to a man who went off to war and never came home. She refused to let it go; that poem was supposed to immortalize him."

Cheryl asked, "Is that what Whisper Park Lane was named after?"

Horace replied, "One and the same; my grandfather was a patient loving man. He kept after her until she finally married him. Eventually she healed from losing Park."

Cheryl looked around the room. "This place reflects so many memories; there must be so much history here."

Horace shrugged. "Only to the family, and right now, that's me."

Cheryl responded, "But if they tear it down, it will be lost."

He replied, "I guess you're right. I had never thought of it that way."

Cheryl asked, "Are your children still living?"

Horace replied, "Yeah, both moved north, one in New York, the other to Chicago. They wanted the excitement of city life; things were just too sedate for them here on the farm. When I pass, they'll just sell this place. My boy comes down about every three or four years, calls a couple of times. I haven't heard from my daughter in a couple of years. I guess I'm just a dotardly old man to them."

Cheryl replied, "Well, I think you're just

charming." She blurted it out before she could stop herself.

Horace gave her a lopsided grin, "Thank you, ma'am."

He poured out tea into a china cup. Cheryl tried to think if she had ever had afternoon tea. It was all quite civilized and yet surreal at the same time; people just didn't do things like that anymore. They sat quietly for a moment while they sipped tea. Barley scratched at the door to be let in. Horace stood and walked to the front door. Barley padded over to a mat by the fireplace and circled, finding just the right spot. He curled up like a giant soft pillow and sighed contentedly; a moment later he was murmuring as if dreaming of hunting rabbits and chasing squirrels.

Horace looked out the window. "This is nice, ma'am. I know you've got a busy life, so thanks for taking time out to visit."

He stood and strode to a closet on the far wall. Inside he removed a sturdy cardboard box labeled *Florida Oranges*. In somewhat shaky hand, "Cher" was scrawled on the side in faded blue ink. He set the carton beside her. "You don't need to take this unless you want to. I can just pitch it if you want."

She regarded the box for a moment. "No. I seem to have shut out this part of my life. It's time I revisit it. Thank you for saving this for me. I would like to go through it, but I won't take up your time doing that here."

She stood and extended her hand. "Thank you for a lovely tea."

Horace shook her hand in return. His voice so low she could barely hear him, he said, "Thank you, ma'am.

Come again any time."

****

She drove for ten minutes on the back road before she saw the first car coming toward her. She maneuvered the gentle curves deep in thought. The box in the seat beside her made tinkling noises, distracting her from her reverie as she drove. The air was crisp enough for her to keep the windows up and sweet enough for her to want them down. Even amidst the glorious yellows of the sweet gum and the ruddy reds of oaks, she couldn't stop thinking about the board hearing the next day. She had never been fired from anywhere in her life.

The feeling crawled over her, casting a shadow on every good thing she had ever done. She envisioned Dr. Wise laughing at her; the haunting image changed to an image of her father laughing at her. She slammed on the brakes realizing she had almost driven through a stop sign. She blinked at the traffic in front of her as it passed. Resolve crept back in. She couldn't do any good by wallowing in self-misery; it was not what she did. She took a deep breath and eased out onto the road; she gave the old Alfa some gas, breathing new life into the engine and into her defense.

Chapter 6

In the professionally decorated room, cherry credenzas dotted the walls with bouquets of silk orchids in different colors. The mahogany board table seated sixteen comfortably, which always left plenty of room for the eleven board members plus the chairman. High back burgundy leather chairs squeaked when sat upon. Each place had a brass lamp lighting the paperwork for each member. It was all very tasteful, it was all very sterile. It was quite fitting for a hospital. This had been the room she had interviewed in with the board; it was the last time she was in this room.

The chairman rarely sat in at these proceedings. In fact, only eight members were necessary to reach quorum. Ray had picked his members well. He and Dr. Wise made the seventh and eighth members, Cheryl did not recognize the other six. She was alone.

Ray asked, "Cheryl, can I get you a glass of water or a soda?"

She returned a thin cordial smile. "No, Mr. Noose; I'm quite fine, thank you."

Gray-haired men in wool business suits and red ties looked down at the paperwork in front of them. A single rawboned severe-looking woman sat on the end closest to Cheryl.

Ray began his pitch to the board. "Thank you for agreeing to attend this special session. Today's meeting agenda will be to review previous performance discussions with Dr. Blumenthal, describe her approach to hospital policy, and the medical decision that led to the subsequent suspension of Dr. Blumenthal's practice at the hospital. The board will render a decision on whether we will continue Dr. Blumenthal's practice at Wise Regional Medical Center."

Cheryl took a deep breath. None of the board members looked up from the paperwork in front of them. Each seemed engrossed like lawyers in a murder trial. Her hands were ice cold despite the comfortable temperature in the room.

The severe-looking woman fired the first salvo. She looked up at her from the paperwork. Her face hard and unyielding, her silver streaked hair tied back in a bun on top of her head. Not a hair was out of place. "Dr. Blumenthal, am I to understand that this is the third time you have gone against hospital policy to treat a patient in a manner that was in direct contradiction to hospital insurance policy?"

Cheryl's voice was flat as she asked, "Could you repeat the question?"

The woman's lips pursed. She looked like she was sucking a lemon. "Is this the third time you've gone against hospital insurance policy?"

Cheryl looked at the ceiling and placed a finger on her lips. She noticed one of the lights over her head was out. Calmly she said, "This is the third time I have used professional judgment to act in the patient's best interest."

The woman's eyes narrowed to slits. "So that's a 'yes'?"

Cheryl looked her in the eye and didn't blink. "No.

I don't believe that's what I said at all; quite honestly, I don't think you want me to use a 'yes' for my response."

The color of the severe woman's face changed from pasty white to pink. Tightly she asked, "And why is that?"

"If my response is 'yes,' then it means the hospital policy does not act in the best interest of the patient. That would directly impact funding from county and federal programs."

The woman looked as if she had been slapped.

Ray intervened quickly. "I think what I heard Ms. White asking was if you were following the hospital policy in accordance with recognized standards of care."

Cheryl raised an eyebrow. "*Whose* standards of care?"

Ray replied, "The hospital's."

Cheryl responded, "If, in fact, we are talking about standards of care, legally they are regionally accepted practices, not just the hospital's. If that is in fact the case, I followed accepted regional protocols for the procedures in question."

Ray responded, "Yes, but were they the hospital's?"

Cheryl pressed, "Show me the standard, and I'll tell you."

Ray sounded uncertain. "Show you the standard?"

Cheryl sat on the edge of her seat, hands flat on the table. "Yes. So far, we have talked about hospital policy. I haven't seen one to date."

One of the gray-haired men sat back in his seat. He tapped his lips watching her. "So you're saying you haven't seen the hospital policy?" He looked at Ray menacingly.

Ray's eyes widened; his face paled. He jabbed at the call button on the center of the table and missed the first time. His fingers trembled as he pressed it. A tinny voice came back through the box. "Yes, Mr. Noose?"

Ray continued, "Clara, could you bring me the written hospital care policy?"

Clara replied, "Right away." The box made a hollow ting as she disconnected.

The gray-haired man looked at Cheryl. "Has the policy been communicated to you verbally?"

Cheryl replied, "Yes."

The gray-haired man asked, "And what did it mean to you?"

Cheryl responded, "That as a hospital representative I was to provide the best care available for the patient."

The gray-haired man asked, "Do you feel like you met the intent of that policy?"

Cheryl spoke with certainty, "Yes!"

Ray squirmed in his seat.

Dr. Wise intervened. "But weren't you warned that you were not following the intent of the policy?"

Cheryl responded, "I was warned to consider the financial side of the policy when implementing the medical strategy."

Dr. Wise asked, "So, wouldn't that mean that you weren't following the intent of the policy?"

Cheryl responded, "I considered it a secondary aspect to the primary policy directive."

Dr. Wise's eyes narrowed. His voice sounded almost sinister as he rebutted, "So, you knew that you weren't following the financial guidelines during these cases."

She sat back and raised an eyebrow giving him a droll look. "Of course, I realized that the procedures were not financially viable, the same as I realize that the three or four cases I treat like this a year do not compare to the thousands that *are* financially viable. I'm not stupid; I know it doesn't cost four dollars for an aspirin."

Venom dripped from Dr. Wise's lips as he asked the next question. "So you feel you're capable of being a doctor and hospital director now?"

She leaned forward, narrowing her eyes. "I think that you would be better suited to be a director than a doctor, as it seems like that's what you're good at, counting pennies..." The words tumbled out before she could stop them.

Ray stopped the verbal affray. "Thank you, Dr. Blumenthal. If you will wait in the lounge, Clara will call you when we're ready."

Clara sashayed into the room. Her blonde hair perfect, her low-cut blouse hefted her cleavage to the forefront. She laid a single sheet of white paper in front of Ray. She grinned at Cheryl. "Hey, Cheryl, I didn't know you were in here."

Cheryl returned it with a thin smile of her own. Clara was quite sweet and quite clueless.

****

She stared at the ugly green and burgundy stripes on the wallpaper and thought how much it made her think of prison bars. The room seemed to close in around her as she sat in the dim light, waiting. The small white refrigerator shuddered loudly as the compressor came on. She picked at the lint balls on her suit, wishing this was over with.

Boomer crashed into the room like he was entering the stadium in front of thousands of adoring fans. "Hey, Cheryl! You're looking a little green; do you want me to sign you out a dose of Phenergan?"

She sighed and brushed her sleeve. "I'm fine. I'm sitting before the board."

He slapped her on the shoulder as if she were a lineman. "Don't worry about them. Throw a few numbers at them and they'll back off."

She didn't respond.

Boomer continued, "Well, I'm off for twelve days. I switched shifts with Rabinowitz and I am headed out of town. Keep 'em straight while I'm gone, you hear?"

Cheryl replied, "Yeah, will do."

****

Clara's sweet face popped into the lounge. "They're ready for you, Cheryl."

She took the ten-mile walk back to the Board Room. Solemn faces greeted her as she entered. She didn't have to hear it. She knew. Ray started his rehearsed dialogue, "Dr. Blumenthal, the board has decided unanimously…"

****

The office reflected old money. Pictures lined the wall of the man seated behind the desk with former presidents. The large cherry desk was scattered with real estate contracts in the millions. Artifacts punctuated the cherry bookcases from Burma, Germany, and Africa. The man behind the desk penciled notes furiously as he thought. His massive hand made the pencil look tiny in comparison. The phone chirped irritating him that he was being disturbed during his "free streaming" thought process. He jabbed the hands-free button on the phone. "*What,* Carla?"

"I'm sorry for the disturbance, sir; there is a Ms. Louise Pope on the phone. She is insisting that she must speak with you."

George sighed. He knew how Louise could be. He was somewhat thankful for it. During a visit to the hospital, she had insisted that he tour the Emergency Room, and specifically, the EKG after mentioning he had indigestion. He didn't know how she knew he was going to have a heart attack, but the attending physician had explained to him that had she not pushed the issue, the resulting heart attack would have most likely killed him or at least seriously debilitated him, because of where it was. She and the doctor had stayed with him all night. They had saved his life. Louise was still a pain in the ass, and always had been. "Put her through."

George answered, "Hello, Louise, how are you?"

Louise replied, "You can dispense with the pleasantries, George. We have a problem with that idiot son of yours."

George responded, "What's he done this time, Louise?"

Louise asked, "Do you remember that nice young doctor who saved your life two years ago in the ER?"

George replied, "Well, of course. How is Cheryl?"

Louise replied, "Terminated."

There was a slight pause while he considered what she said. "You mean, as in fired?"

Louise asked, "Is there any other kind?"

George asked, "Who in blazes did that?"

Louise replied, "Your boy Albert and his little

toadie, Ray."

George responded, "Why, for God's sake? She's one of the best doctors we've got."

Louise replied, "Because she saved a piano player's hand instead of cutting it off, which is what *Albert* wanted to do."

George sighed, "Oh, good heavens. Let me make a few calls and get this mess straightened out."

Louise responded, "Good talking to you, George."

George replied, "You too, Louise."

The line went dead. He sat back heavily into the deep leather chair. He wondered why he had let his wife talk him out of putting that boy in the Marines like he wanted to. The Corps had done a world of good for him at that age. His father had seen to it that he served under the hardest drill instructor in the Corps at the time, Sergeant Cone. He was one hundred and fifty pounds of true blue Marine, had served three tours in Vietnam, and had two Purple Hearts and one Congressional Medal of Honor. His personal mission was to make the Marine Corps proud of his unit—24/7. George had walked tall when he left the unit. There was nothing he couldn't do, no obstacle he couldn't overcome. His son, on the other hand, was a milquetoast. He loved that boy's mother, but she had ruined him, and he had let her do it. It was time to clean up another one of Albert's messes.

He picked up the phone.

Carla answered, "Yes, Mr. Wise?"

George replied, "I need the numbers for Ray Noose at Wise Regional and Dr. Cheryl Blumenthal at her residence."

Carla responded, "Right away, sir."

George stared at the yellow legal pad and his own handwriting. *Develop mining company to mine Helium-3 ore from the moon.* Maybe that was something Albert couldn't screw up.

Chapter 7

Rain poured for days on end; cold, unyielding drops hammered outside. The TV cast an ugly white glare over the dimly lit room as newscasters warned of flash flooding. Foil wrappers and half-finished cereal bowls littered the floor and coffee table. Crumbs covered the floor. Cheryl sat on the couch in a bathrobe eating Rocky Road ice cream and watching the wasteland of daytime drama. She hadn't checked the mail in three days. She hadn't bathed in two. Even the cat wouldn't get near her at this point. There were a dozen messages on the machine. The last one was from George Wise himself. She sighed heavily, realizing she would have to leave her cocoon at some point; she was out of toaster pastries.

The phone clamored again. She considered ripping it out of the wall on her next trip to the bathroom, if she could remember. A small voice came on the other end of the phone. "Hey, Dr. Cheryl, this is Dalton. I'm feeling much better now, and they let me come home. They said you weren't feeling well…"

Cheryl snatched the phone out of the cradle almost without thinking. "Dalton, how does your hand feel?"

Dalton replied, "Oh hey, Dr. Cheryl. You're okay. My hand's okay. It's kind of stiff, but Dr. Wise said it should be okay."

Cheryl asked, "Dalton, this is very important, did

Dr. Wise put your hand in a cast?"

Dalton replied, "Yeah, it's a big white thing. I can see the tips of my fingers though. They look kind of funny."

Cheryl quizzed him, "Can you feel anything in your fingers?"

Dalton answered, "Yeah, they're a little sore, I guess."

Cheryl replied, "Okay. That's good. Dalton, how did you get my number at home?"

Dalton responded, "The nice nurse called Louise gave it to me."

Cheryl replied, "Yes. What a sweetheart she is. Well, Dalton, I want you to put lotion on the tips of your fingers for me. Do you know what lotion is?"

Dalton replied, "Oh yeah, Mom has some."

Cheryl responded, "Okay, well, it was sure nice of you to call, Dalton, and check on me. I've got to run; there are a couple of things I need to do."

Dalton replied, "Okay, talk to you soon."

Cheryl responded, "You bet."

Cheryl's first order of business was to call George Wise. The boy was going to need care. If there was anyone who could make it happen it was George. She didn't care if she had to beg.

****

The phone chirped in George's office.

George picked up the phone. "Yes, Carla?"

Carla replied, "There's a Dr. Cheryl Blumenthal on the line for you, sir."

George responded, "Put her through."

A moment later he heard the line change. He asked, "Cheryl, how are you?"

Cheryl replied, "Good. George, are you staying away from that fatty food?" Once a doctor, always a doctor.

George replied, "Uh, trying to. Say, we've been trying to call for a couple of days now. I'd like to talk over lunch if you have time."

Cheryl asked, "What time?"

George replied, "Twelve thirty is good."

Cheryl asked, "The Copper Kettle good?"

George replied, "Sure, I'll meet you there."

George dropped the phone in the cradle unceremoniously. He liked the girl's style; she was efficient and to the point.

****

The Copper Kettle was mid-town and in full swing when Cheryl arrived. It took her longer to find a parking space than it did to get there. A charming brunette fresh out of high school met her in the front. Cheryl could see her cheek dimple as she smiled on cue. She practically gushed when she found out Cheryl was there to see Mr. Wise. As they walked to his booth, the young woman gushed about how wonderful he was and how fortunate Cheryl was for being seated with him. Cheryl picked lint off her navy-blue business suit as they walked. She had seen the man naked; he was nothing to write home about. They walked past the polished bar with a beaten copper base; neon lights reflected off the polished surface making it look garish in the dim light.

Men in expensive suits drank Scotch and soda and made passes at the cocktail waitresses while they waited for tables. So long as the tips were good, the waitresses didn't care. George Wise never sat at the bar.

The cute hostess led Cheryl straight to him. Everyone here knew him; anyone with any sense feared him. Cheryl was not one of them. He stood as she approached. She grabbed his hand with an uncompromising grip. "Thanks for agreeing to see me, George."

The opening threw him off a bit. He had, after all, called *her*.

George replied, "No problem. I understand there has been a bit of a situation at the hospital."

Cheryl responded bluntly, "I guess you mean the part where they fired me because I saved a boy's hand."

She didn't waste time; he had to give her that. "I guess we're on the same page. You obviously have something on your mind, so let's hear what you have to say."

Their waiter, Ramón, arrived with a ginger ale for George. "What would madam like for a beverage?"

Without looking up, Cheryl replied, "Water, with lemon."

Ramon hovered around George. "Sparkling?"

Cheryl looked up at Ramón. He had big doe-like eyes and full lush lips. His black hair was slicked back. He was painfully thin; the bad boys would love to get his number. "Regular water is fine. Thanks."

Ramon placed his hand on his hip and glided away. Cheryl shook her head and turned her attention back at George. "Look, if the hospital doesn't like the way I treat patients, that's fine. I'll find a practice that does. The issue here is the boy. The surgery was only part of the equation. If Dalton Hope doesn't receive proper physical therapy after his cast comes off, he may not be able to use his hand properly. All I'm asking for is some leniency toward his care. I don't care how, but if I need to work it off pro bono that's what I'll do. This isn't about me; it's about making sure that kid has a fighting chance. If you can't handle that, I'll go to the Channel 32 'Fight for Your Right' group. They eat this public service crap up."

George replied, "Okay."

Cheryl blinked. "Okay what?"

George responded, "Okay, let's give the kid a fighting chance."

Cheryl's eyes narrowed. "This is a child's future at stake here, *Mr. Wise*; I don't appreciate you being flippant about it."

The Marine in him came out. His eyes narrowed as he leaned forward so she could get a good look into them. "I'm not being flippant, Dr. Blumenthal. What I'm trying to say is let's make sure Dalton receives the necessary treatment and care and make sure he can continue to play the piano. You will have that authority as hospital director."

She sat upright. The chair rolled back slightly. Ramón returned with her water and set it on a cocktail napkin. The realization of what George said began to sink in. She leaned forward, placing her elbows on the padded arms of the chair, and laced her fingertips together. Without looking up, she said, "I'm feeling a little frisky today, Ramón. Let's change that to a Sprite with a twist of lime."

Ramón sighed. "Of course, ma'am." Without waiting for a response, he sashayed off.

When he was out of earshot, Cheryl said, "Humph!"

George laughed loudly. It was the funniest thing he

had seen in days. People around them looked up expectantly; seeing George laugh, they went back to their eating.

Cheryl leaned forward. "So, George, I'm a little off my game today. I go from being fired one day to being promoted to hospital director the next. How does that work?"

George took a sip from his cocktail. "We're both adults here, Cheryl. I think it's safe to say that my son, however talented as a doctor, is not CEO material. He doesn't understand the big picture; he's far too interested in his toys."

Cheryl responded, "What about the board?"

George winked at her. "Leave them to me. I'll persuade them to look at the big picture. So, how about you, Cheryl? Can you look at the big picture?"

It was a fair question and one that deserved an honest answer. She regarded him with as much seriousness as she did while she was discussing his imminent heart attack. "George, I will be the best director you have ever seen."

He sat back in his chair and nodded. "Thank you, Cheryl. That's what I needed to hear. It will be a couple of days before the paperwork goes through."

Cheryl narrowed her eyes at him. "So, how *did* you know the boy was a piano player?"

George sat back and took a deep breath. "I spoke to Louise…"

****

Ray squirmed in front of her in a straight-backed wooden chair. He stared across the antique desk at Cheryl who, two weeks before, he had removed from the equation; now she was his boss. It concerned Ray that she had taken a spare office on the second floor, east wing. The office was outdated almost to the point of being austere. She told her staff that she didn't like the old director's office. It was too fancy. He wondered what she thought about his office.

He could feel the tiny beads of sweat on his forehead. Her desk was a mass of papers and reports. It would take days to sort through all of it. She flipped through the papers in front of her, reviewing the admissions stats and hospital fees through outside services. Her brow furrowed as she looked at the expenses, more importantly, the descriptions of expenses. Miscellaneous expense seemed to eat up far more of the budget than building operating cost.

Cheryl sat back in a twenty-year-old office chair. "How long has the hospital Ddrector position been open?"

Ray replied, "Three months."

Cheryl asked, "Who has been acting as the director in the interim?"

Ray responded, "Dr. Wise and I have been dividing the duties. It's been very difficult trying to do two jobs and recruit the proper talent. You must understand it's a very delicate position."

Cheryl understood all too well. The hospital was in trouble, and it wasn't because of lack of funds. "As Mr. Wise has informed you, I am going to fill the role of hospital director until otherwise informed. Dr. Wise has taken a sabbatical to Florida, during which time we will recruit two new staff physicians to backfill his position and mine. I have four candidates in mind; here are their resumés."

She slid four files across the table to him. "I will

maintain a certain case load of patients until we have the other doctors on staff. As human resources director, you will be working with Dr. Rabinowitz, who is our new chief of staff. I will need you to prepare all department managers for an audit in two weeks."

Ray's mouth gaped open. "W-what kind of audit?"

With as much of a poker face as she could muster, she stated flatly, "An accounting audit. I've cleared the cost with George directly. I have hired the accounting and auditing firm of Blankenship and Rice; their team will be here on the twenty-third for two weeks. Everyone will give their full cooperation."

Ray stared at her, his eyes wide. "But that's Thanksgiving week."

Cheryl replied, "I'm aware of that. If our department financial records are ready, it should go smoothly."

The blood drained from Ray's face. His voice squeaked, "I'll make all the necessary arrangements."

She looked down at the folder of paper in front of her. "Great. Now let's go through the staff schedules."

He glanced at his watch. "It's a quarter of twelve. That will take at least an hour; do you want to start after lunch?"

She pointed toward an apple and a bottle of water. "I plan to work through lunch. I have rounds this afternoon."

He sighed and unbuttoned the sleeves on his silk shirt. "We can begin with the cafeteria staff, I suppose…"

****

Marge Hope looked at herself in the bathroom mirror. It had been two days since she quit her job at the Fast and Fresh. Cheryl had offered her a job as the hospital receptionist, which allowed Dalton to stay in the childcare center and almost doubled her salary.

She remembered her last morning at the Fast and Fresh quite clearly; she laid the keys on the counter and told Big Mike, "I quit."

Big Mike sneered at her. "You ain't got the gumption. What are you going to do now, clean toilets at the doctor lady's house? She ain't gonna help you, nobody is. You'll come crawling back to me before it's over. You'll see."

She stood tall a foot away from him and said, "You don't deserve me. You're a mean man and Karma has a way of paying people back." She walked out and never looked back. It took all of her courage to stand up to Big Mike. He was belligerent and a bully. She hadn't really appreciated how much stress she was under until she left. Everything changed for the better after that day.

It was later that afternoon when Cheryl came by reception to see Marge. Marge took great pride in showing her the pictures of Dalton and flowering plants. She placed her hand on Cheryl's. "Hey, Cheryl, are you free for dinner this evening?"

Cheryl looked at her warmly. "I'm sorry, Marge, I'll have to take a rain check. I just stopped by to see how you were settling into your new job. Anything you need?"

Marge looked surprised. "No. I'm still settling in; but I'll let you know if there is anything I need."

Cheryl replied, "Good. My door is always open to you."

Marge beamed. "I don't know what I've done to

deserve this, but I am eternally grateful, Dr. B. If there's anything you ever need, you just say the word."

Cheryl responded, "You just keep things going smoothly down here for me, okay?"

"You have one hundred percent from me, boss."

Cheryl responded, "I'm sure of that."

She made a point to talk to everyone she saw as she walked through the wards. Nurses and staff were happy to see her and wished her well. Department heads gathered in clutches whispering and made furtive glances. As she approached, they scattered like cockroaches in the light. This was not the sort of job where respect was handed out. She would earn it one battle at a time.

In the tiny daycare in the west wing, the children were crammed in a dank waiting room with outdated carpet and a single disinterested warden sitting behind a ridiculously large desk for such a small room. The teenager had stringy blonde hair, poorly drawn tattoos, and a nose ring. She wasn't watching the children and didn't look up as Cheryl entered. Her head lolled back and forth to the beat of a heavy metal band through ear buds, so loud Cheryl could hear it. The girl flipped through the pages of a teen heartthrob magazine.

A ten-year-old boy with a mohawk and a homemade denim vest screamed as he chased another boy with no shirt at all. Cheryl tried to catch him as he went by; he avoided her easily and kept going. A girl in a flowered dress stained with samples of the last ten meals carefully carved a large V in the desk with a rusty utility knife. A tiny blonde girl sat in the corner in a fetal position whimpering. Cheryl tapped the girl with the utility knife on the shoulder. The girl looked up at

Cheryl's outstretched hand and unforgiving eyes. The unkempt child gave her a peeved look but slapped the knife in her hand, almost cutting her with the blade. She retracted the blade and slipped it into her front pocket. She eased toward the inconsolable tike and lowered slowly to her knees. She opened her arms and the tiny girl came to her almost instinctively. Wordlessly, she clung to Cheryl's neck. She could feel the hot tears on her skin. She stood slowly and walked over to the detached teenager; politely she said, "Miss?"

The girl ignored her. Again, "Young lady?"

The girl closed her eyes and went into a drum solo for some unknown tune. Cheryl reached down and unplugged the headset with her free hand.

The girl turned on like Cheryl like a rabid dog. "Hey! What's the deal? Keep your freaking hands to yourself, lady!"

Cheryl still holding the child in one hand asked her calmly, "Why aren't you watching the children?" Dalton stood close peeping out from behind her as he watched the exchange.

The girl snorted. "Like, I *am* watching these little snot-nosed brats. Now if you don't mind, I'll get back to it." She snapped the headset back into the jack.

Cheryl tapped her on the shoulder. The girl put her open palm toward her. Cheryl felt her neck getting hot. She reached over to remove the jack again when the girl caught her hand and squeezed. Cheryl winced. The girl looked at Cheryl contemptuously and let go. Cheryl took a deep breath to avoid saying something in front of the children and left the room. The little girl was holding her with a death grip, and Dalton followed close behind them. They marched down the hall lit only by a flickering fluorescent lamp and stopped at the first phone she could find; they all gathered on a small bench while she called Ray Noose's number.

His salutation tumbled out. "Yes, Ray Noose, can I help you?"

She slowed the conversation down a bit. "Hello, Ray, this is Cheryl. Can you tell me which manager is responsible for the Childcare Center?"

She could hear him take a deep breath on the other end. "Don Reagan, head of radiology, why?"

Cheryl asked, "I need him to meet me down here, please."

Ray replied, "Uh, okay, when?"

Cheryl responded, "Now would be fine, thanks."

Dalton sat beside her. "I know this is better than my old babysitter, but those kids scare me."

Cheryl took a deep breath through her nostrils to calm herself. She envisioned this as a safe place for children, not a factory for potential customers. She sat beside Dalton with the tiny blonde child in her lap. She looked into the little girl's enormous blue eyes while the toddler did not smile but nestled her small head against Cheryl's bosom. They all sat quietly waiting on Reagan to show up. A red-faced little man stomped on the worn burgundy carpet toward them. Cheryl didn't know it was possible to stomp on carpet, but evidently it was.

Reagan was naturally red-faced, and being called down to the daycare made him redder. The red was beginning to crest the top of his bald head as he approached Cheryl.

He wasted no time. "What is so *important* that you had to drag me down here? Just because you slept with

George to get your 'new job' doesn't mean you can boss me around."

Her eyes widened, as did Dalton's. The little blonde girl buried her head in Cheryl's chest further. "Little pitchers, Don."

"What? Do you think I care about these guttersnipes and the janitor's kid? Get over yourself, all right? Now, what do you *want*?"

"These children are not being adequately supervised. I would like for you to find another attendant for the Childcare Center."

"Aw, jeez, woman, I don't have time for this crap."

She held her temper despite the growing urge to slap the contemptuous look from his face. Calmly, she said, "Let's take a look, shall we?"

They walked as a group to the daycare. Cheryl sensed something was wrong, terribly wrong as they approached. The room was deathly silent as they entered. The girl behind the desk looked up smirking. She took her earbuds out.

Don looked at the girl. "Everything okay, sweetie?"

The girl bared her teeth in an attempt to smile. Her braces appeared green in the dim light. "Yeah, Daddy, everything's fine."

The children sat in dead silence not moving a muscle. Cheryl stared in disbelief. She smelled a rat; she suspected it was standing beside her. Don looked at her. "Well? Everything looks fine to me. Are we done here?"

Cheryl's eyes narrowed. "Thank you for your time, Mr. Reagan."

He stomped off. The girl put her earbuds back in.

As Cheryl walked out of the room with Dalton and the little blonde girl still on her hip, she could hear the music. The boy with the mohawk belched as she left the room.

****

Cheryl walked up to the nurse's station with one child on her hip and another so close he looked attached. She pressed her lips together as she walked straight up to Louise. A nurse standing beside Louise nudged the older nurse. The older woman looked up from organizing her charts for the night shift.

Louise arched her eyebrow. "I'm sorry, is being hospital director not enough of a challenge for you? You've decided to pick up some strays along the way?"

Cheryl ignored the jab. "Why is the daughter of the director of radiology working directly for her father?"

Louise replied, "Why are you asking me? I'm just a night shift supervisor."

It was Cheryl's turn to arch an eyebrow.

Louise set the papers down in front of her and sighed. "All right, let's have a consult, while I tell you who's who and what's what."

Cheryl replied, "Let's start with my little friend here." She kissed the small blonde head at her shoulder.

Louise ran a gentle hand through the little girl's blonde hair. "She's Jerry's daughter, day shift housekeeping. Sweet child, but she hasn't spoken a word since her mama died last year."

Cheryl continued, "And the head of our radiology department?"

Louise looked over her reading glasses at Cheryl. "God's gift to Wise Regional, or at least in his mind. He's had every director buffaloed since Mr. Hathecock.

He's been threatening to leave here and go to County General every time someone challenges his authority. Just an opinion, of course, but he seems like a bit of an egotist, if you ask me."

Cheryl tried to keep the sarcasm to a minimum, but she couldn't help it. "What was your first clue?"

Louise pursed her lips.

Cheryl put up her free hand. "Sorry. Why are the conditions so poor in the Childcare Center?"

Louise replied, "Because only the lowest paid employees use it. The others make enough to take their children to a decent day care."

Cheryl shook her head in disbelief. "This place is an administrative nightmare."

The corner of Louise's mouth arched up. "Why do you think I got George to put *you* in the position? It's a win-win for him. If you fail, you're the scapegoat; if you succeed, he's a genius for hiring you."

Cheryl shook her head. "Thanks, I think. Let me get these guys to their proper owners, and we'll talk some more."

Louise responded, "Take your time. I'm here for twelve hours." She looked back down at her paper work.

Cheryl replied, "Louise?"

Patiently, Louise looked up. "Yes, dear?"

"Remind me to *thank* you again for this job."

Louise's snort was deep and resolute. "You're welcome, baby, anytime. I wouldn't have suggested it if I didn't think you were up for the job."

****

Marge looked a little alarmed when Cheryl walked up with Dalton. "Is everything okay, Cheryl?"

Cheryl disarmed her anxiety with a grin. "Of course. I decided to visit Dalton and look at his hand. Since it was so close to quitting time, I thought I could save you some time and walk him up here."

Marge looked relieved. "That was so nice of you. Are you sure you can't come over for dinner tonight?"

She gave Dalton a small hug. "I'd love to, but I am swamped here. I'll catch up with you guys soon, I promise."

She exchanged a knowing glance with Dalton. "Keep up the good work on the therapy with that hand, sweetie."

He grinned broadly. "Sure thing."

****

Cheryl could see Jerry's face tighten as she walked toward him with his daughter on her hip. His knuckles were white on the mop handle by the time she reached him. "Uh, hello, Dr. Blumenthal. Is something wrong?"

She responded carefully, "I happened to be in the Childcare Center and couldn't help but notice your daughter crying. I asked if I might be able to visit with her a little before it was time for you to go home for the day. She is such a sweet child."

He looked like he was going to cry. He held out his hands. The small form reached out to him and wrapped her tiny arms around his neck silently. "Melody is daddy's little angel. She's just had a bit of a rough time lately."

Jerry held Melody. His large raw-boned hands gripped the child tenderly as she nestled against his gray uniform. He continued hesitantly, "I lost my wife, Linda, almost a year ago to an aneurysm and Buster two months ago."

Cheryl blinked. "Buster?"

Jerry nodded. "Yeah, ol' Buster was a golden retriever; gentlest dog around kids ya ever seen. He got cancer a couple of months ago, and he was gone in a couple of weeks. She just kind of shut down after that; I can't seem to do nothing to help her. Linda's sister comes down from Hinton, West Virginia, about once a month, but I think that just confuses her somehow."

An idea came to Cheryl as she replied, "We're going to take good care of her. Give me a couple of days, all right?"

Jerry answered, "Yes, ma'am. Thank you. But, uh, ma'am?"

Cheryl asked, "Yes, Jerry?"

Jerry asked, "Did you intend for me to keep Melody until shift change?"

Cheryl suddenly felt about five inches tall. "I'll have her in my office, East Wing, Room 700."

Jerry handed Melody back to Cheryl. "Thank you ma'am, for everything."

****

Rays from the late day sun cast an amber hue on the ancient frosted glass in the office. The vinyl cushion groaned and hissed as she placed the small golden child on the comfortable worn couch that had been in vogue two decades earlier. Gently she covered the small body with the softest blanket she could find and tucked a tiny pillow under the blonde curls. In the dim light, Cheryl caught the merest hint of a smile on the small cherubic lips which dissipated like smoke in the wind a second later. Her eyes closed, and she was soon fast asleep.

Cheryl plopped in her desk chair and yanked the tarnished chain of the banker's lamp on her desk hoping it would come on. It did, flooding the office with the sudden glow of a sixty-watt bulb. She flipped through the dangerously overstuffed Rolodex trying to find the right number, vowing silently to update the contact list on her phone someday. After a second pass through the disjointed system, she finally found the address of one Amit Patel stuck to Allied Movers by some unknown brown gravy-like substance. She pried them apart and plucked Amit's card free of its paper prison. She jabbed the hands free button and listened to the satisfying sound of a dial tone before she dialed the number.

It rang only once before there was a click on the other end. "Mercy Hospital Radiology, this is Amit."

His voice conjured up memories of late-night study sessions, obscenely entertaining poker games, and impromptu bashes that kept them sane amidst the pressure of med school.

"So, what does a girl have to do to cash in on some long overdue favors?"

She could hear the light chuckle on the other end. "So I suppose this means I need to plan for a road trip?"

****

Don waited with infinite patience. He remembered the delicious anticipation as he watched his small furry pet tarantula feed for the first time; this wait was almost as good as that time.

He thought about the morning he picked up Muerte from the Pets to Go in the bustling little Careway Corner strip mall. Wedged between Erma's Crafts and The Gun Show, they had a rather brisk business. It smelled different from other pet stores; they made no attempt to hide the odor of death and decay, which permeated the shop. It was utterly perfect. He carried

Muerte out into the bright sun and rising heat of an unusually warm June morning. His new pet seemed quite content in his small acrylic box; he never moved a muscle as Don loaded him carefully into the front floorboard of the Beemer. It had been one month since he walked into the store and ordered the Mexican tarantula; it seemed like it had taken longer.

His prize waited as well; he rested in his small box on his desk. Don sat quietly and tapped his finger as he reflected on the first time he dropped a small white mouse into the glass box. He had shivered with eagerness as he waited to see the first kill; the clear domination of a superior species as it exercised its evolutionary superiority. For days he watched; for days nothing happened. At some point, he began to feed the mouse, for fear it would starve to death. The small white mouse gained confidence and began to approach closer and closer to the spider. Eight dark eyes regarded its quarry coldly, dispassionately, and seemingly quite disinterested. After three days, Don was concerned that his prize was sick or perhaps dying. Maybe it was the wrong type of mouse. Maybe, maybe, maybe…

On the morning of the fourth day, he sat at his desk patting the new hair implants affectionately, as one might pat a small dog. He inspected the small nodules in a hand-held mirror, smiling at the thought that he would look twenty years younger in a few weeks. He diverted his attention from the mirror to the clear acrylic box on his desk. It happened so quickly, he almost missed the sudden eloquent precision of the kill. In the blink of an eye, powerful front legs secured the unsuspecting white mouse while powerful mandibles clamped the tiny rodent in a strangle hold, suffocating it; the small fleshy pink tail spun like a tiny dervish as it squeaked in horror and was silent. The powerful spider held it patiently waiting for it to suffocate; the hairs on its abdomen bristled momentarily in the heat of the kill. In less than a minute it was over, the small mouse lay limp and the spider began the slow process of ingestion. He shivered remembering the thrill of it. So now Don waited with the patience of Muerte for his quarry. Cheryl would be here soon, and his plan to take her down would be equally exquisite.

****

It was nine thirty a.m. sharp when the buzzer on her phone went off. The office was so quiet the sudden noise almost startled her. She pressed the button. "Yes?"

Marge replied, "There is a Dr. Patel here to see you, Cheryl."

Cheryl replied, "Thanks. Could you bring him up?"

There was a slight pause. "Right away."

Cheryl glanced at her watch to see how much time she had before her next appointment. She cursed silently when she realized she only had fifteen minutes. It would take her at least twice that long to get the material ready for the meeting. The phone rang again. She tried to ignore it, but it blared at her again. Irritated she jabbed the button. "Yes?"

There was a moment of silence on the other end before Marge squeaked. "Cheryl, I have a State DHSR inspector here. He's here to investigate a complaint."

Cheryl paused for a moment. "I'll be right down."

Chapter 8

He introduced himself as Chris Ross, DHSR, field investigations. He was not what Cheryl expected. He was a small man with thinning blond hair. He had a certain illusion of ineptness that quickly dissipated when he began asking questions. Ray, Cheryl, and Mr. Ross sat around a small oval table in her office while he asked questions about restraints, drug protocols, and RN supervision.

By the end of the day, Cheryl was emotionally drained. Mr. Ross planned to return the following day for interviews and a walkthrough. Ray would take point for walking him through the hospital. This was not his first audit.

The accounting audit was three days away. The staff team was preparing their department reports. As a contracted audit, there would be a cost associated with delaying the auditors from visiting. This was becoming a delicate balancing act.

Amit sat in the lobby. Patiently. Cheryl stopped. Her head dropped when she saw him. Amit arched an eyebrow and asked, "Can I buy you some dinner?"

She raised her head. "That would be nice."

****

It was dark when they arrived at her apartment. The meal had been relaxing at the nicest restaurant in Center Point. The two teenage boys down the hall were having another epic stoner party, and the door stood open to their apartment. Music blared, and two teenage girls hung off the bannister shouting profanities to a third below in the parking lot. They all laughed as mindless teenagers do.

Amit watched as Cheryl fumbled with her keys on the door. "You're a doctor. Why do you live in this place?"

She raised her eyes up to him. "Student loans. Med school wasn't a free ride for me."

His eyebrow furrowed. "I thought you had scholarships."

She didn't meet his eyes. "For most of it, yes. Not all. I'll be paid off in a couple of years."

Amit asked, "I guess you live in this place until then?"

Cheryl dismissed the tone of the question, "It's not so bad. The neighbors are okay except for the boys down the hall. And they're not mean, just kids with no direction other than living in the moment. Some days I envy them."

Amit looked surprised. "Envy? Them? How so?"

She gave him a tired look. "We're a lot alike, you and me. Driven, results oriented, focused. Those kids live in the moment. Have we ever done that?"

An impish smile crossed his lips. "There was that one time with Jell-O shots at the Delta house."

She raised an eyebrow. "Once a decade does not qualify as spontaneous."

Max meowed loudly as soon as she entered the apartment. She dropped her case and proceeded to the kitchen. She opened a cupboard and pulled Max's cat food out. As she tried to pour his food into the bowl,

Max practically pushed her hand out of the way almost making her spill the food on the floor. She gave him a long stroke. He purred loudly as he devoured the cat chow.

She moved back to the small living room. Amit was sitting comfortably on the couch. She sat close to him. Her hand rested on his knee.

He said, "I really missed you."

Cheryl looked into his deep wonderful eyes. "I missed you too."

Her hand began to trace up his leg. Amit shifted uncomfortably. "There's something you need to know."

Cheryl stopped. There was something in his voice. He cleared his throat. "I have a girlfriend."

Cheryl removed her hand. "Oh, I'm sorry. I didn't mean to come on so strong."

Amit replied, "It's okay. There is no way you could have known."

Cheryl's voice was low as she replied, "Is she pretty?"

He responded facetiously, "No. She has the face of a horse." He rolled his eyes. "Of course, she's pretty."

Cheryl replied, "I see. Aside from that, how would you feel about moving to Center Point as the head of our radiology department?"

Amit responded, "I'll think about it."

Cheryl pressed. "I could really use your talent."

There was a tinge of irritation in Amit's voice, "This is a big move for me. I have a lot of opportunities at Mercy that you can't offer at Wise Regional."

His comment stung. "I understand. Just promise me you'll think about it."

Amit replied, "I will."

****

The forecast was bleak. Rain dripped from the eaves, and Cheryl stared at the ceiling. She felt embarrassed. Even more so than when she was put on administrative leave. Not only had she been rebuffed by her former lover, her backup plan to face Don Reagan in radiology had fallen through. She pulled herself together. The DHSR investigator would have little concern for her personal woes. It was time to put on her game face. Max rubbed up against her. An affectionate scratch behind the ears was all she had time for.

The office was buzzing with activity when she arrived. The mounting rainfall outside did not seem to dampen the electricity in the air. The lights were on in the small anteroom outside her office. Don Reagan sat with his arms on the chair and his index fingers resting on his lips. As Cheryl approached, he rose. His suit was tailored and expensive looking. He looked like a made-man from the movies. "A word, Dr. Blumenthal?"

She relaxed her face, showing as little emotion as possible. "Certainly, Don. Please step into the office."

They had barely cleared the threshold when he dropped an envelope on the desk.

She looked at him civilly. "What's this?"

Don replied smugly, "My resignation. I've had offers from County General for years. Your little stunt in the Childcare Center the other day made me realize that Wise Regional is not somewhere I want to remain affiliated with."

Cheryl replied, "I'm sorry you feel that way, Don."

Don's reply was terse, "It's Dr. Reagan, thank you. I expect a full outplacement package from you as per the hospital policy."

Cheryl looked at him wearily, "I'll have Ray process it as soon as he can."

Don replied, "If I don't have it in two days, my lawyer will contact you directly. I'm not a person to be trifled with, Dr. Blumenthal."

Cheryl did not goad him into a verbal altercation. "I'm sure you can see yourself out, *Don*." She turned her back and began unpacking her bag. She paused and glanced back at him over her shoulder.

He stood for a moment. His lips were tight. A small vein on the side of his head began to throb. He stormed out of the office.

She closed the office door. She dialed the nurse's station at the emergency room. A bright voice greeted her. "ER, this is Ann."

Cheryl was relieved. For everything that Louise was, Ann was not. Louise was a drill sergeant. Ann had the soothing calm of an angel. "Hi, Ann. This is Cheryl."

"Well, hey, Cheryl. It's so good to hear you. I haven't seen you since your new appointment. How's that going?"

"Great, thanks. Ann, could you tell me something?"

Ann replied, "Sure, hun, what do you need?"

Cheryl asked, "If you really needed to get something done quickly in radiology, who would you call?"

Ann responded without hesitation, "Honestly, if it was me, I would call Darlene. I know Don is in charge, but Darlene really runs the department. She has for years. My two cents."

Cheryl replied, "Thanks, Ann. I owe you a coffee."

Ann responded, "Tea, hun. Red Rose preferred. You take care, okay?"

Cheryl replied, "I will. You too."

She hung up. This would have to be quick. Ray wasn't in yet, and she needed to ensure there was a department structure in place. She picked up the phone again.

"Radiology, this is Maurice."

"Hi, Maurice. This is Cheryl Blumenthal. Is Darlene around?"

Maurice replied, "She is, ma'am, but she's in the middle of something. Can I have her call you right back?"

Cheryl responded, "No need. I'll take care of it. Thanks."

She dropped her coat and headed to radiology by way of HR.

****

Ray was just settling into his office when Cheryl arrived at his doorway. He looked up. "What's wrong?"

She shut the door behind her. "Don Reagan resigned this morning. I don't think we have the luxury of time to find a backfill for him. I would like to suggest Darlene Johnson as his temporary replacement. What do you think of that?"

Ray replied, "I like Darlene; she shows a lot of initiative. I think it's doable."

Cheryl responded, "Good. Go ahead and work up a temporary memo to the team, and I'll go talk to her. I'll close with you when it's time to circulate. Does that sound like a plan?

Ray replied, "Yes. I've got it."

She turned to leave but stopped. She turned to face

Ray. He looked up expectantly. What happened next obviously shocked him by the look on his face. She extended her hand. Hesitantly, he raised his hand to meet hers. She responded with a firm grip. "I want to thank you for your professionalism through everything that has happened over the last month. I know this has been a difficult period in the hospital's history. You and I have had our differences. Through it all you've maintained an admirable level of decorum."

Ray blinked. Cheryl knew it was the last thing he would have expected. It was common knowledge that he had worked for this hospital for eight years with virtually no feedback from the directors. This was a first. "Thank you, Cheryl. I'm glad you're pleased with my performance."

She replied, "Rougher seas ahead. Let's keep our eye on the horizon, shall we?"

He smiled at the nautical metaphor. "Yes, ma'am."

****

Darlene's eyes were focused on a spreadsheet as she spoke on the phone with the service provider. "You sent us the wrong solution base. We caught the mistake when we ran our quality test. I need the correct solution today. I don't need excuses! If you can't deliver, I'll have you replaced as a provider. Are we clear?" There was a short pause. "Thank you." She slammed the phone down. She sensed a presence behind her. She whirled around to find that she was face to face with Dr. Blumenthal. "You heard that, I guess."

Cheryl's face was stoic. "I did."

Darlene continued, "I promise you I wouldn't have threatened those idiots at Forest Medical if they hadn't made a mistake and tried to blame it on our testing process."

Cheryl asked, "How serious was the mistake?"

Darlene replied, "It wasn't bad. It would have caused a failed test, but not put anyone in danger, physically."

Cheryl probed a bit deeper. "What if the test had resulted in a false negative? And we didn't identify the root cause during the first round. What then?"

Darlene paused for a second. "Oh. I hadn't thought of it that way. That could have been more serious than I thought. I guess I wouldn't be so upset, but this is the fourth time this quarter they have sent us the wrong batch. I spoke with Dr. Reagan about this, but he says every provider goes through cyclic trends like this and he would take care of it."

"Darlene, that's why I'm here. We need to discuss something. Can we speak in private?"

Darlene was surprised with the politeness of the request. "Certainly, Cheryl."

Cheryl closed the door to the small office. "Darlene, I like your instincts. You don't need to use me as a hollow threat. If this is a real problem, then let's talk about solutions."

Darlene asked, "What about Dr. Reagan?"

Cheryl replied, "Dr. Reagan is no longer with Wise Regional. He resigned this morning. I've talked to Mr. Noose in HR. He agrees that until we find a director for radiology, you will be the acting supervisor. What do you think of that idea?"

A lump formed in Darlene's throat. She tried to fight back the tears but could not. They streamed down her face. She quickly wiped her eyes and held herself erect. "Ma'am, no one has ever given me an opportunity like this. I know it's temporary, but I will give everything I have."

Cheryl replied, "Thank you, Darlene. Call me if you have any questions or issues."

Darlene stopped her. "Cheryl?"

Cheryl responded, "Yes?'

Darlene asked, "What about Forest Medical?"

Cheryl asked, "Do you have a qualified provider in mind?"

Darlene nodded. "Yes, ma'am. Duluth Scientific has better pricing and more rigorous testing processes."

Cheryl replied, "See procurement about changing providers. And track the cost savings for me in a spreadsheet if you can."

Darlene responded, "No problem."

Cheryl shook Darlene's hand. "Welcome to the management team."

****

It was day two with DHSR. Today Mr. Ross would assess the documentation the hospital kept on various topics. Since the investigation was specifically directed at patient care notes, he was going to focus on the pharmacy and the nurse's orders. Tomorrow, he would begin the three-day process of interviews with the staff. Ray was responsible for the entire process. Ray set up an interview room where he and Mr. Ross could talk privately with staff members. Mr. Ross would continue until he was satisfied that he had sufficient context for the hospital. The process was structured and intense.

Cheryl was still in damage-control mode. With Don Reagan gone, she had also lost her Childcare Center's daytime worker—Don's daughter. Cheryl was running out of options. She needed someone she could trust…and fast.

Cheryl waited while the phone rang several times. "Hello?"

"Horace, this is Cheryl Blumenthal. I need a big favor…"

Chapter 9

Less than an hour had passed when Cheryl's office phone rang. Marge's voice sounded confident. "Hi Cheryl. There's a man, a Mr. Peebles, here to see you."

Cheryl replied, "Thank you, Marge. I'll be right down."

Marge poked her over the phone. "You *promise?*"

Cheryl laughed. "Yes. I promise that I won't leave him sitting in the lobby like the other gentleman."

Marge replied, "All right. We'll see."

Cheryl wondered if she had created a monster.

Horace met Cheryl in the lobby. Barley was at his side. A guitar hung from his back. "I was surprised to hear from you, Cher. Good surprised, but surprised."

Her eyebrows knitted together. "Horace, I wouldn't ask this if I didn't think it was possible. Our Childcare Center attendant has left without warning. We have four or five older children who could certainly use your special touch. It would only be for a couple of days until we can find a replacement. We can't pay much, but I'll try to see if I can make it worth your while to come in."

Horace replied, "Cher, I don't need money. And as for the kids, I never get a chance to see my grandkids anymore. This would be a treat for me. It's either this or sit around and stare at ol' Barley here all day." Barley looked up and wagged his tail at the mention of his name.

Cheryl squeezed Horace's arm. "Thank you, Horace. There's a very special girl I'd like for you to meet."

****

It was lunch on the second day of interviews with DHSR. Cheryl entered Ray's office. Ray's lips were thin, almost white. His eyebrows furrowed as he looked up. He kept his voice low.

"They have found several concerning discrepancies with the pharmacy records. The rest of the findings are easily resolved. Some RN certifications that haven't been updated in the files, but the work has been completed. The primary complaint was by a family member that their son was restrained without due cause. After Mr. Ross reviewed the case file, he considered it unfounded. The patient was admitted by the police due to some lacerations and became combative. There were good case files for that one. The issue with the pharmacy is something different. Could you shut the door?"

The door clicked behind Cheryl as she eased into a chair. Ray continued, "There were several instances where Boomer signed out painkillers for patients that were not in his case file. They were narcotics."

Cheryl's brow knitted together. "Can you give me an example?"

Ray shuffled papers and pulled out a case report from the pile in front of him. He began to read. "Eighty-six-year-old female admitted due to a complaint of labored breathing. History of CHF. Examination concurs the presence of pulmonary fluid. Given intravenous diuretics to shunt fluids…"

Cheryl prompted, "Sounds pretty straightforward."

Ray replied, "There is no record of the attending ER physician, Peter, prescribing painkillers, and yet Boomer signed off on the order."

Cheryl's face clouded. "That makes no sense."

Ray's brow was still furrowed. "We have three other cases we've found with similar findings."

Cheryl responded, "This could cost him his license."

Ray nodded. Cheryl continued, "What is Ross's perspective on this?"

"He admitted it looks bad, but he's willing to give us time to conduct an internal investigation. It is a clear violation based on their statutes. It will go on file as a violation, but we will be given the opportunity to develop a corrective action plan and a closure date. We'll have thirty days. Boomer will have to go on administrative leave and will not be allowed to contact any of the pharmacy staff during the review process. The board will have to decide on the best course of action."

Cheryl considered the options. "Do we have the option of hiring a third-party investigator?"

Ray looked up and paused for a long second before responding. "I hadn't considered it, but that's a really good idea. Do we have anybody like that around here?"

Cheryl replied. "As it turns out, we do. I treated a female patient about six months ago for appendicitis. Her husband runs a small investigation firm and alarm company here in town. I'll reach out to him."

Ray responded, "I'll close with Mr. Ross this afternoon. He's wrapping up his preliminary findings, and we'll have a closing meeting this afternoon with him."

Cheryl asked, "What time?"

Ray replied, "I'll try for three thirty."

Cheryl responded, "I'll make some calls."

****

The phone rang only once before a woman's voice answered, "Ironsides Security, how may I help you?"

"Good afternoon, my name is Cheryl Blumenthal. I'm the hospital director at Wise Regional Medical Center. Is Mr. Ironsides available?"

The woman replied, "Well, hey, Dr. Cheryl, this is Hazel. You treated me for appendicitis. Do you remember me?"

Cheryl responded, "I sure do. How are you?"

Hazel replied, "I'm doing great now. I can't thank you enough for taking care of me, like you did. I'll see if Dwight's around. Can I put you on hold?"

Cheryl responded, "Most certainly."

After only a brief pause, an authoritative voice responded, "Dwight Ironsides, how may I help you?"

Cheryl replied, "Hi Dwight, this is Cheryl Blumenthal. I might need to hire you."

****

They sat in the board room with the entire staff. There was an unusual silence in the room. Ross began with a well-practiced monologue. "As a representative of DHSR, I would like to thank you for your cooperation in this investigation. We began with three complaints, and two have been resolved. The third will need further investigation and resolution pending a follow up by DHSR."

When the meeting with Ross concluded and Cheryl had walked him to the door, she returned to her office and sank back in her chair for a moment. Feelings of self-doubt tried to churn forward. *Was she up for all of this?* She pushed the thought back. The worst that could happen was that they would fire her, again. She regarded the thought of this grimly. In the meantime, she had a hospital to run. She rose from her chair and headed to the Childcare Center to check in on Horace and the kids.

She walked the hallway deep in thought. As she approached the Childcare Center, a faint sound made her pause. It was singing. Curious, she moved closer.

"Froggy went a courtin',
Do da, do da...
Froggy went a courtin'..."

The first glance made her catch her breath. The children formed a circle around Horace who sat in a straight back wooden chair. At his feet sat Melody, her small arms hugging Barley's neck. The dog's tail thumped the floor in rhythm to the music. The look of happiness on her small face brought a tear to Cheryl's eye. It was by far the most glorious thing she had seen in a long time.

Chapter 10

James burst into Cheryl's office. "I don't know what to say…it's just…it's been so long…"

Cheryl stood. "James, if this is about…"

She didn't finish. He moved so quickly she had no time to react. He caught her in a bear hug and squeezed. He let go and backed away with his eyes still alight. "I'm sorry, ma'am, but the most wonderful thing happened last night. My baby girl asked me for a Happy Meal."

Cheryl replied, "Sometimes it just takes the right circumstances to help children…"

He interrupted again. "No, ma'am, it takes the right people. I owe you, ma'am. Anything you ever need, you just call. I'm your man. I got my baby girl back; there ain't no price tag for a thing like that."

She replied, "I agree." He left the room as quickly as he entered.

She sat heavily back in the chair. There were some things you are never prepared for. Spontaneous gratitude was one of them.

****

The phone buzzed. Marge's voice was very businesslike. "Dr. Blumenthal, there are three people to see you from Blankenship and Rice."

"Thank you, Marge. I'll be right there."

For weeks they had been preparing for the

accounting audit. Cheryl had communicated to the staff that the focus was Sarbanes-Oxley compliance, the reality was she could sense something was wrong with the hospital's finances, but she couldn't put a finger on it. And she was not an accountant. It would take her months to uncover the problems, if she ever did.

In the privacy of her office, Cheryl looked Kelly Masters in the eye and said, "I can see we are having financial problems at the hospital; what I can't see is where the problems are. I am approaching this from a top down perspective. Start with the financial statements by the board and directors and work your way to the physical accounting. Does that make sense?"

Kelly replied, "Perfectly. We have helped many organizations like yours find opportunities for compliance and sometimes restructuring opportunities to help leverage your assets more effectively."

Cheryl replied, "Good. We're on the same page. Where do we start?"

Kelly removed a template from her case. "Here is a structured process for us to follow. It is a checklist that the firm has developed to make the process we follow systematic and repeatable. We'll start with the chief financial officer."

Cheryl led the team to the accounting department. Daniel Case met her at the door. Daniel was the accounting supervisor. He was clearly uncomfortable with what he was about to say. "Dr. Blumenthal, Delores Smythe called and took a personal day this morning."

Cheryl's eyes narrowed. She refrained from saying what was on her mind. "Daniel, do you think you can help Kelly and her team?"

She could see his face turning red. "Yes, ma'am. I'll do what I can."

Cheryl responded curtly, "Thank you. Do everything in your power to support this team. They are here to help us. We'll have a wrap-up meeting at the end of the day."

She looked at Kelly. "Is four thirty okay?"

Kelly replied, "We'll provide you with a summary of what we reviewed today and what we'll need for tomorrow."

Cheryl responded, "Great, I'll meet with you here in the accounting department." Cheryl turned an about face as she tried to curb the rising tide of anger.

Ray sat in his office organizing the documents from the DSHR investigation. Cheryl entered and closed the door behind her. He looked up. She wondered if he could see the fire she felt burning her eyes. He put his pencil down and sat back. Cheryl took a deep breath before she spoke. "How many meetings did we have with staff to prepare for the accounting audit?"

Ray replied, "Two per week for the last three weeks, barring the last four days with DHSR."

Cheryl fired back, "Precisely. Delores is not here today. Her department is principal in the audit. Did she call you?"

Ray hesitated before he replied, "I haven't heard anything from her, no."

Cheryl was direct with Ray. "You tell me. Is there a good reason why I should not be pissed?"

Ray sat quietly waiting for her next statement. Cheryl narrowed her eyes. She put both hands on Ray's desk and leaned over. Ray swallowed hard.

Cheryl asked, "Should I call her?"

Ray replied, "She works for you. From a professionalism perspective, she should have provided you with a heads-up that she wasn't going to be here. Did she call Daniel?"

Cheryl responded, "She called him to say she was taking a personal day. If she's taking a personal day, somebody had better have died in the family."

Ray coached her, "Cheryl, remember we need all the facts before we jump to conclusions. Hear her out."

Cheryl straightened up. She sat down in one of Ray's plush chairs. "I'll try to keep my tone in check."

He raised an eyebrow. "Are you sure you can make the call without losing your temper?"

She looked at him levelly. "No. But I'm pretty sure I can make the call without putting this organization in jeopardy of a lawsuit. Is that acceptable?"

Ray shrugged. "I guess it will have to do. We can't just let something like this go. Remember, try to keep an open mind. Maybe it is something legitimate."

Cheryl's face was unemotional. "Your optimism is appalling."

Ray put the phone on speaker and dialed Delores's number. The phone rang several times before being answered. "Hello?"

Cheryl asked, "Is this Delores?"

Delores replied, "Yes. Who is this?"

"Hi, Delores. This is Cheryl."

"Cheryl who?"

Cheryl took a deep breath. "Cheryl Blumenthal, from Wise Regional Medical Center."

Delores responded, "Oh. What do you want?"

Cheryl felt an involuntary twitch in her eye. "I'm

sorry to bother you at home, but we started the Sarbanes-Oxley compliance audit today. You're a critical piece of that process. You aren't here today, so I wanted to check and see if you were okay."

Delores replied, "I'm fine. I decided to take a personal day today. It's been really stressful at work lately with all the additional tasks."

Cheryl made a face at the phone, but continued civilly, "I can appreciate the stress you've been under. And I would like to thank you for all the effort you've put into the planning, but right now is when we need you the most."

Cheryl heard a drawn-out sigh over the speaker. "Oh, very well. If this is so important to *you*. I guess I can reschedule my manicure for another day."

Cheryl's eyes grew large. Ray wondered if she was going to explode. Cheryl kept her cool as she responded, "Thank you, Delores. That is very helpful for the hospital."

Delores replied, "Whatever."

Cheryl kept her tone in check. "We'll see you when you can make it in." The phone went dead on the other end.

Cheryl looked at Ray. "I just keep telling myself, I took the Hippocratic oath, I took the Hippocratic oath…"

Ray tried to be empathetic, but he was as stupefied as Cheryl. "I would like to offer you some sage words of advice based on my years in human resources. But to be honest, I've got nothing."

Cheryl sat for a moment calming herself. Ray tried to change the focus a bit. "Do you think Daniel has everything he needs, or do we need to give him some administrative support?"

Cheryl thought for a moment. "Let's see how we do today, and I'll ask him after the auditors have left."

Ray replied, "Good plan. When Delores gets here, let's meet in my office. I'll do the talking; that keeps you from getting upset again. We need you calm, cool, and collected. Everyone is looking to you as the example. If they see you stressed out, then they will be stressed out. Does that sound all right to you?"

There was wisdom in what Ray said. "You're right. I won't lose my head."

Cheryl stood to leave. As she put her hand on the doorknob, she turned. "Thanks, Ray. I guess I let my emotions take over for a bit."

Ray smiled. "It happens to the best of us. There are a lot of things I wish I could undo in my life. Putting you on suspension is one of them. I let the board influence me, but I should have stood my ground. I can't fix that, but I can keep us from repeating the same mistakes. Delores will have to answer for this, but now is not the time. We'll deal with this when the time is right."

Cheryl replied, "You're right. Call me when she gets here."

****

It was close to two o'clock when Delores arrived. She was a tall attractive brunette with deep brown eyes. The meeting was short and painful. Cheryl met with Delores in Ray's office. She began, "Delores, I know audits can be stressful. However, this is one where we have invited in the auditors to help us understand how we can streamline our finances a bit."

Delores looked at Cheryl. Her mouth had a slight

frown. "I don't understand all this rigmarole. Dr. Wise always helped me with what we needed to do. Why don't you ask him?"

Cheryl cocked her head slightly. *Could Delores be that clueless?* "Dr. Wise is on sabbatical in Florida. He won't be back for several more weeks." She tried to keep her tone gentle. "Delores, you are the financial director. This is *your* responsibility. This is what we pay you for."

Without warning, Delores burst into tears. "It's just too much. It's all too much! With all the land and expansion and big plans, I can't do all this!" She vaulted from the chair and ran from the room sobbing.

Cheryl started to rise, but Ray motioned with his hand and went after Delores himself. Cheryl shook her head and sat back heavily in the chair. What Delores said made no sense. They were in the middle of a financial crisis. It was Delores who was supposed to have a handle on the balance sheet. It didn't appear that she had any idea what she was doing. Cheryl stood, straightened her skirt, and walked out of the office. Like Ray said, they would handle this later.

Daniel was working with Kelly in his office. The table looked like someone had dumped a box of papers and walked away. Pages were perilously close to falling on the floor. Cheryl hoped this was not a sign of how the audit was going. Kelly looked up. Her expression was somber. She looked back at Daniel. "Let's take a break."

He sat back and breathed a sigh of relief. "I could use a coffee. I'll be back in a few minutes."

When Daniel left the room, Kelly shut the door behind him. "Cheryl, you did the right thing by calling us in. Daniel is trying his best, but it's evident he's overloaded."

Cheryl asked, "What do you mean?"

Kelly responded, "He is trying to manage accounts receivable, accounts payable, tax depreciation, payroll, you name it. Even with all that, it appears there are gaps between what is coming in as revenue and what is going out in invoices. By all accounts, you should have a balanced financial sheet. But it's not. We still have a lot of digging to do."

Cheryl asked, "Are there any indications of land purchases?"

Kelly shook her head. "It's too preliminary. I don't see anything yet. There is a lot to sift through here. It will be a couple of days at least. What about Ms. Smythe? Will she be helping us with this?"

Cheryl replied, "I don't believe she will be much help. It appears she was getting help from one of our resident physicians, who is away on a trip right now."

Kelly responded, "That's a problem. We'll meet at four thirty today, but I won't have much to review with you."

Cheryl stood and shook her hand. "I understand. This is day one, and we have a hill to climb. Thank you for all the hard work. Let me know what I can do to help."

Kelly's expression was stoic. "I will." She returned to the mound of paper on the desk.

An hour and a half later, Cheryl sat with Kelly in her office, the door closed. The paper avalanche had followed her. Kelly donned a pair of glasses and a pencil protruded from behind her ear. The legal pad in her hand was covered in scribbled notes.

Kelly opened with, "I have good news and bad news."

Cheryl braced herself.

"The good news is I believe we understand why the hospital is having financial difficulties. The bad news is the hospital is very close to defaulting to Chapter 11."

Cheryl gasped. "Bankruptcy?"

Kelly nodded. "Yes. Unfortunately, that's not all. It appears that some transactions which occurred are several years old and have had a snowball effect on the balance sheet. It has been carefully managed over time up to this point."

Cheryl sat back. Her index fingers rested on her chin. She wondered if her actions as a doctor had contributed to the problems the hospital was having. She braced herself for the answer. "Is this because we've taken on medical cases that were denied benefits under low-income health-care assistance?"

Kelly shook her head. "No, not at all. Your claims and balance sheet from government income look good. Your income from the Fed looks a little too good. It's interesting, because the question you asked earlier today made me look a little more closely at another area."

Cheryl replied, "Go on."

"It appears that the hospital made several land acquisitions. It appears that cash loans were taken out by the hospital to buy land under a balloon payment schedule, which you are now repaying. The land was in turn sold to a holding company at a loss. In short, the hospital is repaying loans for property it does not own."

Cheryl puzzled over this information. "Can you explain to me about the balloon payment first?"

Kelly looked up from her legal pad. "The hospital gave the land owner earnest money up front, and then obtained a loan from the bank to pay the balance. The hospital has been making interest payments for the last three years which are supposed to mature into a balloon payment to the bank for the balance of the amount. What I can't seem to find a record of is where the money from the sale of the property went."

Cheryl's jaw dropped. "How is that even possible?"

Kelly sat back. "The method is somewhat irregular, but not unheard of. Because the hospital is private, you're not required to go through public disclosure, so the way this was done is still a mystery. So far, I've not uncovered anything illegal, but it's certainly not a good financial practice. It is very close to embezzling."

"So who signed off on all this?"

"It appears that Ms. Smythe signed the paperwork."

Cheryl sighed. "Do you think there is more to this?"

Kelly's shrugged. "I can't say. What I can say is that, historically, when we uncover something of this nature, there are several layers of irregularity that mask the root causes. We won't have any evidence without some research. It could take days or weeks to find other issues."

Cheryl responded, "I understand. How soon can you write your formal report?"

Kelly scratched her head. "For what we've found so far?"

Cheryl answered, "Yes. I need to present this to the board."

Kelly paused before responding carefully. "Considering that we do not understand the depth of the issue yet, there could be a broader implication with who was involved."

The cautious approach made sense. *What if there were board members that were involved?* Cheryl replied, "You're right. At a minimum, I've got to tell Mr. Wise. He is the hospital benefactor."

"I appreciate the position you're in. But please make sure he understands this is a preliminary finding. We may find other evidence that would change the direction of our investigation. If we do find evidence of deliberate illegal activity, we are required to report this to the appropriate agency by policy."

Cheryl looked at her notes before looking at Kelly. "I understand. I'll phrase your findings carefully."

Kelly left. Cheryl sat for a moment contemplating how to break the news to Mr. Wise. She looked out the window. A cold hard line of clouds laced by the colors of the setting sun foretold a change in the weather. She picked up the phone to call George.

Chapter 11

The night before, the call with George had gone smoothly. Cheryl had focused on the message that the hospital was in financial trouble, and the team was continuing to analyze opportunities to bring the hospital back into the black. She avoided the language around the potentially fraudulent activity that his son might well be a part of. Cheryl knew better than to present a problem that she did not have all the facts on yet or a path forward on fixing the issue. She would have to be patient and wait for Kelly's analysis. On a brighter note, George had invited her to a pre-Thanksgiving cocktail party at his home. It was the first cocktail party she had been invited to in, well, *ever*. She even considered going shopping for a new dress.

Boomer burst into her office. "Cheryl, I swear to you, I never issued any drugs that I wasn't supposed to!"

She motioned for him to sit. "First off, welcome back from vacation. Second, let's talk about this with Ray."

Boomer placed both hands on her desk. "Am I in trouble?"

She looked him in the eye. "The hospital is in trouble. You have been implicated. We need to understand this. The best way to do that is for all of us to be honest with each other. So, I'm going to ask you once; I need you to be completely honest with me. Did you sign out narcotics for patients that did not require them?"

He put his hands together as if praying. "No, I swear to you, absolutely not."

She stood and looked at him somberly. "Then let's figure out what *is* happening."

A few minutes later, they gathered around the small round table in Ray's office. Several brightly colored files littered the table with papers scattered in all directions. Cheryl, Ray, and Boomer had been putting the pieces together for over an hour.

Boomer sat back and shook his head. "I don't understand. It's my signature, but I swear I haven't heard of some of the patients."

Ray tried to be helpful. "You see a lot of patients on rounds. Is it possible you forgot?"

Boomer sat back. "No. That can't be. I remember my patients. It just doesn't make sense." He sat back and picked up the log in front of him. His finger traced the entries and stopped at the date: 10/13. Boomer stabbed his finger at the date in front of him. "There! That can't be!"

Both Cheryl and Ray looked around to Boomer's side of the table. Cheryl asked first, "What? What did you find?"

"This date. It shows that I signed out Oxycodone to a forty-three-year-old patient who was admitted due to trauma from an automobile accident—patient was complaining of back pain."

Ray shrugged. "Sounds normal enough. What's so special about that entry?"

Boomer looked up with fire in his eyes. "That was

Friday the thirteenth. It was the day of my son's homecoming game. I talked to my son about not believing in superstition and to just play hard. They won that night by a landslide."

Ray looked at him expectantly. "So I'm not quite sure I understand."

Boomer reached over and took him by the shoulders. "Don't you see? I was supposed to work that night, but I traded out because I wanted to see my son play. I wasn't even here that night! I couldn't have signed out anything."

The implication hit all three of them at the same time. Someone was forging Boomer's signature. Now they needed to know who. Cheryl knew it was time to bring in Dwight Ironsides, the private investigator.

****

Dwight Ironsides would be there later that afternoon. Cheryl needed a moment to think. Between the financial audit and the DHSR investigation, she needed help keeping everything together. The hospital needed some tight supervision, and she was stretched thin with few people to trust. She needed help. The phone broke her train of thought.

"Cheryl Blumenthal."

Marge's voice sounded bright and cheery. "Hi, Cheryl. There's a Dr. Patel here to see you."

The statement threw her off. *Amit? Why was he here?* "Thank you, Marge. I'll be right down. I promise."

She heard Marge chuckle. "I'll hold you to that."

Amit stood tall smiling as she entered the lobby. "Cheryl, can I take you to lunch?"

It was only eleven o'clock, but it was a welcome

distraction. It was a good time to hit the Copper Kettle.

The hostess wasn't at her station yet, so Ramón seated the couple. It was clear Cheryl was almost invisible to Ramón, who could not take his eyes off Amit's perfect cheekbones. Cheryl rolled her eyes. *Good grief.*

Amit laughed when Ramón walked away. "Don't be angry. It happens all the time."

She gave him a curious look. "So why the surprise visit?"

Amit replied, "I owe you an answer."

Cheryl began, "Look, it's okay—"

He raised his hand and cleared his throat before speaking. "I have something I need to say."

She sat back, not knowing what to expect next.

He began, "We were very close during college. You were one of the few people I could talk to. When we graduated, you shut me out. I don't know why. I can't have a one-way relationship. Does that make sense to you?"

The statement hit her hard. Cheryl didn't have many friends because she was afraid that a relationship would end up like her parents. No one had ever forced her to look at herself in that way. She felt the lump rise in her throat. She swallowed it back down. She would not cry in front of Amit. In a small voice, she responded, "Yes."

He kept talking. "I have taken a great chance coming here today."

She asked, "How so?"

Amit replied, "I broke up with my girlfriend, and I have resigned at Mercy. I am willing to take the job here, if it is still open."

This time, she couldn't hold back. She grabbed a linen napkin and covered her face as the tears came out. He tried to reach out, but she waved him away. Brokenly, she asked, "Are...are you saying...what I think...you are saying?"

He smiled. "Yes."

Ramón showed up with the drinks. She hastily wiped away her tears and regained her composure. She ordered a Caesar salad. It was all she could think of.

Cheryl dropped her head and spoke into her lap. "I don't mean to be distant. I had a really screwed-up childhood."

He reached across the table and lifted her chin. "We all had screwed-up childhoods. It's okay." She expected angels to sing behind him.

She pulled herself together. "So, I guess you are asking for a job? Is that what I'm hearing?"

Amit took a sip of his drink and replied, "I believe that was the implication, yes."

In a businesslike voice, Cheryl asked, "Do you have any references?"

Amit's face was impassive as he replied, "One. A certain Dr. Cheryl Blumenthal."

Cheryl responded, "Can this Dr. Blumenthal be trusted?"

Amit replied, "I certainly hope so. If not, I'm in deep trouble."

A thought came to her. "So, do you have a tux?"

For the first time, he looked surprised. "Huh?"

Cheryl arched her eyebrow wickedly. He would make nice arm candy at Mr. Wise's party.

****

The meeting with Ray, Darlene, and Amit went

hurriedly. She explained to Ray and Darlene that Amit was a candidate to fill the radiology director position. Darlene was to take Amit on a tour. They would meet later that afternoon.

As Darlene and Amit were leaving, Dwight Ironsides was waiting outside her office. Ray led Dwight into the office and closed the door behind them.

Cheryl began, "Dwight, thank you for coming. We have a bit of a situation at the hospital that we need to investigate carefully."

Dwight sat erect, a small notebook in his hands for details. "So, tell me all the facts. Don't give me any supposition, just what you know."

For thirty minutes, Ray and Cheryl tag teamed Dwight on the DHSR investigation, the details of the complaint, and the findings by the investigator. Dwight listened attentively, only occasionally stopping them for clarification.

Finally, Dwight responded, "You have a couple of options: one, we can put an undercover person on the inside of the pharmacy department. That person would wait and try to catch the person you suspect of forging signatures; this will take some time and may or may not produce a suspect. Or two, we can interview some people. I have some very skilled interviewers that could probably narrow the list of people to the point we could be very targeted in the investigation. This would take a few days, versus a few weeks with the undercover investigator. It's risky, because people may not admit anything."

Cheryl looked at Ray. "What are your thoughts?"

Ray thought for a moment. "I would suggest interviews. It's less risky, and if people found out we were putting undercover investigators in the pharmacy department, we would have a human relations nightmare on our hands. No one would trust us."

Dwight nodded in agreement. "That is a drawback of the strategy."

Cheryl looked at Dwight. "I would agree that interviews are the best way. We could also use this as objective evidence with DHSR. How soon could you start?"

"We will need some time to review the logs, schedules, and evidence to find a pattern. Plan on three days. In the meantime, we need to corroborate the information you have absolving the accused doctor and validate the possible cause. No offense, but the doctor in question could be lying. We need to confirm his alibi."

Cheryl looked at Ray. "Can you help him with the files?"

Ray stood. "Absolutely."

As they left the office, Cheryl noticed she had mail in her inbox. As she leafed through the envelopes, she noticed a letter from Dr. Wise. Curiously, she opened it. Her eyes narrowed on the statement "I do hereby resign my position..."

It was becoming a trend.

****

Kelly Masters sat across the table from Cheryl and Ray. Her hair was a tight bun. Her tone stayed neutral as she recited a complex rendition of lies and deceit. She systematically dissected the hospital's finances with remarkable precision. The only difference between Kelly and Cheryl was that Kelly was not there to save the patient—only to determine why the hospital was dying.

It took over an hour for her to reconstruct what she had found, but there was key evidence not available to her. She only had half the story. There were holding groups and banks outside of the hospital that were partners in the duplicity, but there was not a clear trail of names to follow. The perpetrators had hidden their tracks well. The people most implicated were gone or untraceable at an accounting level. Because the hospital was privately backed with no oversight by larger publicly held institutions, Kelly had little to pursue. She confirmed the original suspicion that a series of bank notes and shorted loans had almost crippled the hospital's finances, and there was evidence of unprecedented salary increases for a small group of staff members, two of whom were Dr. Wise and Dr. Reagan. Conveniently, both had resigned. There was no direct evidence of embezzlement, but just shy of it.

Cheryl contemplated the situation. She was a captain of a sinking ship. There were too many lives to save with too few lifeboats. She would have to do something creative.

Cheryl waited until Kelly was finished speaking. "So, do we have options available to resolve this?"

Kelly was cautious in her reply. "It is possible to use Chapter 11 to manage creditors, but that creates its own set of problems. The key for you is to determine what happened to the money that was supposed to buy real estate. I don't have any authority to go to the other institutions involved and probe; that is outside my domain. I can't advise going to the authorities on what I have, but I can say their view may be different than mine."

Cheryl replied, "I understand. Thank you, Kelly."

When Kelly was out of the room, she turned to Ray. "I'll have to tell George. I'm going to wait until after the party if you feel it's appropriate."

Ray was thoughtful. "I think that is wise. It's likely both Albert and Don will be at the party. It would cause some unnecessary drama."

Cheryl replied, "I agree."

****

Amit waited patiently for Cheryl outside her apartment. She was nervous. She didn't know if the formal gown was too much or too little. She did know it looked great on her as Amit's eyes widened as she approached his long sleek German sedan. He vaulted from the car and opened the door for her. It surprised her. They had been friends for many years. This was the first time he had ever reacted like that.

As they cruised down the highway, she couldn't resist asking Amit an awkward question, "Do you miss your girlfriend?"

He gave her a sideways grin. "Sometimes. She was a phenomenal lover. But quite honestly, she was only interested in me because I was a doctor. I was a trophy boyfriend. We didn't really talk about anything of substance. Weather, sports, fashion, and so on. She was as dense as an axlewood tree. She has already started dating one of my friends from cardiology. Fortunately for her, he has a Porsche and a one-track mind. She probably thinks she got an upgrade."

Cheryl replied, "I doubt that. So enough about Bambi. The people you're meeting tonight are the power structure behind the hospital. No pressure."

Amit replied, "I've got this. I can hobnob with the

best."

The car approached the Wise estate. Its enormity caught Cheryl off guard. The broad circle drive led to marble columns and a balcony overlook. The lawn was pristinely manicured and uncharacteristically green for this time of year.

As they were preparing to pull into the gated drive, a small pickup cut in front of them shooting up the drive. Amit jammed on the brakes causing them to lurch forward in the seats. Cheryl's eyes were wide as the truck bounced past them and careened precariously onto a service road and out of sight around the house. The back was a combination of primer spots and rust. A peeling bumper sticker on the back read *This Vehicle Insured by Smith and Wesson.* Cheryl wondered, *Why?*

They eased forward to an awaiting group of red-coated valets. The young man on the passenger side opened Cheryl's door, while the second valet opened the driver's door for Amit. At the expansive double doors entering the mansion, George and Charlotte Wise met them with hugs and smiles. Cheryl had never met Charlotte. She was a vivacious middle-aged woman. A debutante in her earlier years, now a thriving socialite. Her thick blonde hair framed azure blue eyes and ruby red lips. Her red silk gown accentuated with a lace bodice was flawless for the occasion.

Cheryl and Amit followed the path to the ballroom where servers carried trays of Dom Pérignon. Frescoes climbed the walls with floral vines tempting the eye to greet the cherubs overseeing the room. Cheryl, transfixed by the ornateness of the room, didn't notice that the dinner guests' conversation had stopped. All eyes turned to Cheryl and Amit as they entered the room.

Cheryl noted the murmur as people stared at her. She sensed the charged atmosphere in the room and smiled charmingly to dismiss it. Cheryl picked up a glass of champagne.

Amit whispered in Cheryl's ear, "Problems?"

Cheryl looked up from the bubbly. "Jean Toomer once said, 'Fear is the noose that binds until it strangles.' I suspect some of the guests are beginning to feel a tightening at the neck."

Amit looked at her, concerned. "What do you mean?"

Cheryl replied, "I'll tell you later. George will be in here soon; the tide will turn, you'll see."

Cheryl worked her way through the room, introducing Amit with grace and poise.

George and Charlotte glided into the room in perfect sync. All eyes were on them. George raised a toast, "To my friends, and soon-to-be friends, enjoy the moment, and enjoy your evening!"

All glasses raised and the guests sipped their champagne. The mood in the crowd shifted. People began to mingle, voices raised, loud raucous laughs filled the room, and champagne flowed freely as servers hurriedly moved about capturing empty glasses and replacing them with full ones. Cheryl nursed her wine frugally. She had never been a wine drinker. Bourbon, on the other hand, was a different story.

Cheryl whispered into Amit's ear, "I'm going to take a powder."

Amit blinked. He had lived in America for years. He still did not appreciate all the nuances of the English language. "I'm sorry?"

Cheryl sighed. "I'm going to the bathroom, assuming I can find it."

Amit replied without smiling, "Oh good. I'll be sure to run off with the first harlot who speaks Hindi."

Cheryl gave him a subtle jab to the ribs. "Very funny."

Cheryl maneuvered through guests smiling as she made her way to the red door along the wall. The short hall led to the kitchen. The kitchen was immense, easily the size of her whole apartment. In the corner, Charlotte had two scruffy young men cornered at an industrial size stainless steel refrigerator. The young man closest to Charlotte wore a grungy T-shirt, and his long greasy hair, goatee, and cobra tattoo with dripping fangs on his neck seemed uncharacteristic for the setting. She was leaning toward them. While Cheryl could not make out the words, the tone was unmistakable. She was not happy. Cheryl cleared her throat.

Charlotte Wise whirled around. Her eyes were wide with surprise. She quickly composed herself and flashed a dazzling smile. "Why, Cheryl, how delightful! How can I help you?"

Cheryl responded in like. "Is there a powder room close by?"

As soon as Charlotte turned, the young men fled the kitchen out the back door. Through the large window, Cheryl could see the battered truck that almost struck Amit as they had come in. The two, rough-looking young men climbed in it.

Charlotte gently took her arm. "I must be losing my touch. I haven't shown you a thing about this humble house of mine. Come along, dear. I'll show you to the powder room."

Charlotte continued to hold her arm as they walked. She chatted on, "...and the caterer wanted to charge me for uniforms. I told him, if they were going to nickel and dime me to death, I would just go look for someone else. You know, he changed his tune in a New York minute..."

Cheryl made a mental note that she did not have the capacity to fathom the worries of the rich.

She returned to the main hall to find Amit chatting comfortably with Albert Wise about polo matches in India. The hairs on the back of her neck stood up.

Albert Wise smiled at her broadly as she approached. "Well, hello, Cheryl. How are you?"

A smirk on Amit's face indicated his clear enjoyment of the awkwardness of the situation. *He's enjoying this!*

Cheryl flashed a beautiful smile. "Lovely, thank you. Just lovely."

Dr. Wise replied, "Why, as a matter of fact, yes you are. I don't believe I've ever seen you so radiant. In fact, I didn't know you owned anything but scrubs."

All the while thinking what a cheeky cretin Wise was, she bit her tongue to keep from saying, *Well, there was that one time you tried to get me fired; I was wearing a business suit then.*

Instead, Cheryl asked, "How was Florida? It must be wonderful this time of year."

Wise's brow furrowed for just a moment before he recovered, remembering his lie. "Oh, just grand. Tampa is wonderful this time of year."

It was a bad lie. Even Cheryl had seen the news where they had suffered a late season tropical storm. The devastation was in the millions. At least she knew that if she were to play Wise in poker she would clean him out.

George tapped a crystal goblet with a spoon, old school style. "Ladies and gentlemen, they are ready for us in the dining room." George lumbered back in the direction they came in. People fell in tow.

The dining hall was larger than the ballroom. Sculpted columns punctuated the walnut panels along the walls. Blooming vine frescoes adorned the ceiling encircling the two crystal chandeliers over the table. The assigned seats positioned couples across from each other. An army of servers stood at attention along the walls waiting to serve. Cheryl panicked when she observed the main course was to be prime rib. Amit didn't eat beef. She spied some pheasant under glass and relaxed.

The entire Wise family was seated at the opposite end of the table along with Don Reagan and his wife. Cheryl could now understand why Don's daughter was so detached. Don patted his new hair implants while his wife pushed her lips out with her tongue. She was a cross between a largemouth bass and Goth gone wrong. Her low-cut black dress accentuated her surgically enhanced bosom, which distracted Cheryl only slightly from her expressionless Botox face. Cheryl immediately averted her eyes to keep from staring.

Cheryl sat between Coleen Kiser and Alexis Megalos. Both were delightful older women, who, like Cheryl, were invited as a matter of politeness and not of worthwhile desire to have them attend. Sitting between the pair turned out to be one of the liveliest experiences Cheryl had been a part of in a while.

Alexis' bubbly personality stood in stark contrast

to that of her husband, who sat meekly beside Amit. She launched into a story about her grandson. "And the little scamper picked up the cat, carried her to the toilet, and by the time I got to the bathroom, the cat was howling like a banshee, all four paws spread-eagled on the toilet seat and Dom—that's my grandson—was laughing trying to shove her in."

Cheryl chuckled. "And why was he trying to put the cat in the toilet?"

Ms. Megalos laughed. "That is precisely what I asked him. He said the cat was washing herself, and he thought he would help her, and the toilet was the closest thing he could find that was his height. Anytime he comes to the house now, Mum Mum—that's the cat—hides under the couch and growls at him."

Amit smiled. "I can't say that I blame Mum Mum one bit."

Alexis took another sip of Dom Pérignon. "I know, right?"

Coleen chimed in, "You wouldn't believe what my little Jeremy did the other day. The little snot decided he wanted one of the new piglets our sow dropped for a pet. He went into the pigpen, picked up one of the piglets, and started to run. The old sow took out after him. Jeremy was screaming, the piglet was squealing, and Papa was yelling, 'Let the pig go, boy!' "

Her husband, Harold, nodded at the account but never stopped his methodical attack on his plate of hors d'oeuvres.

Coleen continued, "Jeremy finally dropped the piglet and the sow stopped chasing him, but Jeremy was still running full speed at the fence. At the last second Papa reached down and grabbed him up over the pen."

Alexis laughed. "Do you think he learned anything?"

Coleen rolled her eyes. "He informed us that pigs might be too big, so he's going to start smaller. He's been eyeing the chickens. Papa keeps the gate locked on the chicken coop, just in case."

They all laughed merrily. Cheryl caught a glimpse of Don Reagan's wife raising an eyebrow at them, or at least, that's what Cheryl thought she was trying to do through all the Botox. They chatted through the soup, salad, prime rib, coffee, and desserts. It was all quite lovely. The ladies made Cheryl promise to visit for a play date in the future.

Charlotte Wise walked to the end of the table and joined the conversation. "So, girls, did I hear you planning a play date?

Coleen smiled politely. "Why yes, Charlotte. Would you like to come?"

Charlotte grinned broadly. "Why, of course, darling. Let me know when, all right?"

The evening began to draw to a close, and Cheryl excused herself with Amit. She waited for an opening with George and Charlotte. George's nose was red and eyes a bit glassy. He pumped Cheryl's hand vigorously. "Thanks for coming, Cheryl. Fine job at the hospital, fine job."

Cheryl smiled. "Thank you for putting your confidence in me."

Charlotte hugged her. "So how is your accounting *thing* going, dear?"

The question caught Cheryl off guard. She replied carefully. "Our research is going well. We have identified several opportunities that will help us put things in order."

Charlotte gushed. "Wonderful! I'm sure things will work out just fine."

Cheryl replied, "Thank you."

One of the young men at the door retrieved Amit's car within moments, and they were on their way. Cheryl turned to Amit. "Care for a night cap at my place?"

He arched an eyebrow. "Sure."

****

Max the cat meowed around their feet as soon as they walked in. Cheryl reached over, scratched him behind the ears, and led him to the kitchen for some kibble. She called to Amit as she went. "Make yourself comfortable. Why don't you try to find something on TV?"

Cheryl detoured to her bedroom and made a quick change into her faded red State T-shirt and sweat pants. She let her hair down. When Cheryl stepped back into the room, she noted that Amit had thrown his coat and tie across an oversized chair. He was settled back into the plush couch.

She handed Amit one of the two gin and tonics with lime she carried in as she nestled next to him on the couch. "So, what are we watching? Nothing serious, I hope."

Amit replied, "Nothing serious, I promise."

With a bright flash of orange, the announcer spoke in a gravely somber tone. "*Next on WWC, Earthquake-Aggedon Four, the day the earth wouldn't stay still, starring Vin Johnson as Reagan Rexrath and...*"

Cheryl gave Amit a long sideways look. "Really?"

He laughed and took a sip of his gin and tonic.

"Yes, really."

Cheryl's hand rested on Amit's leg.

"Oh, Reagan, how are we going to get out of the reactor core?"

"Hold tight, Mindy, my bullwhip should reach that stair bannister."

Cheryl snuggled in closer to Amit. Her hand moved to his belly. He dropped his arm around her shoulder pulling her in tighter against him.

"Oh, Reagan, you're so strong. Why did I ever leave you?"

Cheryl took Amit's hand and kissed his fingers gently.

"Mindy, we both made mistakes. We need to put that behind us now, before the next aftershock hits."

Amit lifted Cheryl's head up and kissed her deeply. He tasted sweet, like gin and pheromones.

"Quick, Mindy, grab my belt as we swing over the chasm."

Cheryl and Amit slid over on the couch. She lay on top of him. She nibbled at his neck.

"Reagan, is that your nightstick?"

"For Heaven's sake, Mindy, what else would it be?"

Cheryl and Amit's clothes lay in a debris field across the room. Max peeped out from under the *State* T-shirt on the floor. He rolled over in the shirt and meowed.

"Hold on, Mindy, here comes the next aftershock!"

Mindy screamed, "Oh my God, Oh my God, Oh my God!"

Cheryl kissed Amit on the lips and got up. "I think our drinks need a refill."

Amit's hair was matted in sweat and pointing in fifteen different directions. He had a lopsided dazed grin. "I would agree. And some oxygen if you have it."

Cheryl laughed and padded to the kitchen. She stopped and turned back to Amit. She asked coyly, "Is there an Earthquake-Aggedon Five?"

Amit's eyes widened a bit. "Good God, woman…"

Chapter 12

The crisp voice on the other end of the line answered, "Ironsides Investigations, how can I direct your call?"

Cheryl responded, "Hi, Hazel. This is Cheryl Blumenthal. Is Dwight there?"

Hazel changed her tone a bit. "Well, hey there, Dr. B! Dwight's here; let me get him for ya."

Moments later, Dwight's gravelly voice was on the other line. "Hi, Cheryl. How can I help you?"

Cheryl carefully worded her response. "Dwight, do you have any experience in tracing financial irregularities?"

Dwight chuckled. "Do you mean embezzlement, Cheryl?"

Cheryl would not drop her guard just yet. "Well, let's say we found some documents indicating loans were made, and the money that was borrowed can't be fully accounted for."

Dwight sighed. "Cheryl, if you want me to help you, you're going to have to tell me more. I can't investigate what I don't know. But in answer to your question, yes, I have forensic accounting experience."

Cheryl paused for a moment. "Can we meet for a coffee or something? I don't want to bring you here, but I can't do this over the phone."

She could hear Dwight leafing through paper.

"Sure. I'm open this afternoon. What about three?"

She scribbled the note on her desk plotter. "Great. How about Dot's Diner?"

Dwight responded, "That works. I'll see you there at three."

****

Cheryl drove home at lunch and hastily changed into blue jeans and a sweatshirt. She didn't want to stand out. There was little chance of running into the hospital staff at Dot's. It was frequented by truck drivers and the occasional bar fly.

Dwight was already in the diner with a cup of coffee when she arrived. As Cheryl slid into the aging booth, the waitress sashayed up. She wore a blue uniform with coffee stains and pink bunny slippers. "Hi. My name's Maggie. What'll it be, hun?"

Cheryl looked up. "Coffee. Black."

As Maggie wandered off. Cheryl removed a folder with the case files and an executive summary from Kelly Masters. She looked Dwight in the eye. "Dwight, I am way out of my element here. I don't know how to approach this. I need someone objective to help me understand if I'm seeing fraud or not."

Dwight replied, "Let's see what you have, and we'll go from there."

Cheryl slid the file over to him. He opened it and began to read. Maggie sloshed over a cup of coffee toward Cheryl, almost drowning the file. Dwight snatched it up, keeping it out of the line of fire. He glared at Maggie who took little notice, as she was looking at Cheryl.

"Y'all having anything to eat, or what?"

Cheryl responded calmly, "Do you have pie?"

Maggie never changed her posture. "Best dang pie in the county. Today we have lemon chess and Dutch apple."

Cheryl replied, "Dutch apple, please." The statement made her pause. This was the place her Dad always brought her after they went fishing. She always ordered Dutch apple. She twinged a bit at the thought of it.

Dwight didn't look up. "None for me."

Maggie swayed back to the counter. She reminded Cheryl of a Jersey cow from the backside.

She turned her attention back to Dwight. He held the file without putting it back on the damp table top. "Cheryl, based on what you have here, it looks very much like you have a serious embezzlement case. I believe I could help with verifying some parts of it, but ultimately it needs to be investigated as a criminal matter. On the surface, there appears to be some collusion on the part of the bank. Because banks are regulated by the Fed, I would recommend that we reach out to the FBI. I happen to know a field agent in the Raleigh office who can help with this type of case."

Cheryl sat back hard. She took a deep breath. *The FBI...this would be a difficult conversation with George.* "Why do we have to involve the FBI?"

Dwight answered, "Because the bank crosses state lines as a matter of business, the FBI will have jurisdiction. We could start with the local police department, but they would ultimately have to turn it over to the FBI."

Cheryl nodded absently in agreement. Maggie showed up with the pie. The aroma was enticing, but Cheryl had lost her appetite. This had suddenly turned very serious. She responded, "I'll have to let George know first."

Dwight replied, "That's understandable. Do you need me to help with that conversation?"

Cheryl thought for a moment. "I think that would be best. I'm a doctor, not a lawyer."

Dwight responded, "I'm no lawyer, but I've been an investigator for a long time. You've uncovered something here that is very subtle. It would not have been easy for most people to recognize this. It was good insight on your part to pursue this. It would be a real problem for the hospital later if it's not corrected. Plus, it covers you in case someone else were to discover it."

Cheryl replied, "I know. But it feels like the situation is out of control."

Dwight patted her on the hand. "It is, in a way. But by doing the right thing, you can bring it back under control. There are people counting on you and your staff. I know; I was one of them. In the end, it will all blow over. You'll see."

Cheryl's jaw was tight. She finally looked at Dwight and said, "I'll call George and set up a time."

Dwight stood to leave. "Call Hazel and set it up. I can move my schedule around if you need me to."

Cheryl's lips were thin. "Thanks, Dwight. I really appreciate it."

He patted her on the shoulder. "No problem. You'll get through this. I promise."

She stabbed the pie with a fork. It didn't seem to taste as good as it had when she was a little girl sitting across from her dad.

****

Cheryl and Dwight met with George in his office

downtown. George had converted an old Victorian house on the edge of the business district in Center Point. The dark wood trim, high ceilings, and gold relief wallpaper made Cheryl think of the Biltmore house. The room smelled of cigar smoke, but George didn't smoke around Cheryl if he thought better of it. He reviewed the assessment in front of him. Every now and then he would grunt to himself as he read something that disturbed him. "Much of this predates Lester leaving the hospital. Do you remember Lester leaving, Cheryl?"

Cheryl nodded. "Yes. Lester Rosenthal. I remember he left quite suddenly."

George looked at her over his reading glasses. "That's the understatement of the century. He left a typed resignation on his desk, stating he left for personal reasons and left his keys on top of the envelope. We never saw him leave and didn't hear a thing from him about his final paycheck."

Dwight spoke. "That is odd. It almost sounds like he was trying to disappear. I can run a credit history on him to see if he shows up anywhere."

George looked at Dwight. "If it helps explain any of this, I'd say yes. But let's see if your friends at the Bureau go down that path."

Dwight nodded.

Cheryl spoke up. "So this means you approve of me going to the authorities?"

George's eyebrows furrowed. "As much as it pains me to say it, yes. We can't afford to risk the institution's reputation by trying to sweep this under the rug. Especially if there are other institutions involved like the bank. Because of my association with the hospital, it could open me up to scrutiny in my other businesses. While I'm not hiding anything, those kinds of investigations make my customers nervous in all my business interests. I could stand to lose millions if this got into the wrong hands and my competitors leveraged it to gain customer confidence. I have just signed a contract in the aerospace sector of my business that is lucrative and very volatile. I can't afford an implication of impropriety."

It occurred to Cheryl that George had a lot to lose if this wasn't handled correctly. The thought made her pause. This could lead to a substantial loss for George. The pressure was on her to ensure this was handled correctly.

The air was uncomfortably cold in the drizzling rain as Cheryl left George's office. She pulled her coat collar up against the chill. George's instruction had been clear. Bring in the authorities but make it discreet. He couldn't afford to have the press getting wind of this. Dwight and Cheryl would drive to Raleigh together to meet with Agent Burns. The appointment was in three days.

Cheryl drove back to the hospital. She was in a daze. As she entered the lobby, Marge Hope rose from the desk and came around to greet her. Her eyes had tears as she greeted Cheryl. Cheryl snapped back to the reality of the moment. "Marge, what's wrong?"

Marge dabbed her eyes. "Nothing's wrong. It's all good!" Cheryl looked confused.

Marge replied, "I'm sorry, Cheryl, it's wonderful. Today, Dalton played the piano for the first time since the accident. It was beautiful. It will be a while before his hands are completely healed, but you couldn't tell it.

My boy can play again."

Cheryl hugged Marge. "He's a sweet boy. He deserves the best."

Marge looked at Cheryl. "You never lost faith in us. I don't know how to repay you."

Cheryl responded, "It's simple, Marge. Never feel like you don't deserve happiness. Dalton is a wonderful boy. You're a great mom. You can repay me by living your lives to the fullest. Don't lose your faith. Can you do that?"

Marge squeezed. "You're the best person I've ever known. I don't know what I would have done without you."

Cheryl replied. "Marge, seeing Dalton play will mean more to me than you can imagine."

They parted, but the encounter eased Cheryl's anxiety about meeting with the FBI. In the context of hospital director, this was about doing the right thing.

Chapter 13

Cheryl was lost in thought as she walked to her car. The meeting with the FBI was in two days, the closure plan had been submitted to DHSR on the pharmacy issue, and Horace had organized an event to repaint the Childcare Center. She paid little attention to the footsteps behind her. She stopped at her car and pulled her keys to unlock the door. Suddenly she was smashed into the side of the car. She felt the weight on her back as someone pressed against her.

His breath smelled of cigarettes and coffee as he hissed into her ear. "Stay away from them Feds, if you know what's good for you."

Cheryl was too stunned to speak or move. He had a strong grip as he pinned her arms to the car.

In the distance, she could hear a man yell, "Hey! You leave her alone."

Suddenly the pressure was gone. She turned to see her assailant running toward a dilapidated truck. Jerry ran past her with a tire iron in his hand. The hoodlum jumped into the truck. It roared to life and peeled out with remarkable speed for its condition. Jerry threw the tire iron at it, which clanged loudly as it landed in the bed of the truck as it sped away.

He stopped and walked back toward Cheryl. "Are you okay, Dr. B?"

Cheryl straightened out her coat and took a deep

breath. She gave him a brave smile. "I'm good, Jerry. Thanks to you. I'm not sure what would have happened if you hadn't come along."

He stood next to her. "Ma'am, you really ought to report this to security, maybe even the police."

She considered the implications of both. Her assailant was clearly trying to scare her away from the meeting with the authorities. Which meant she had touched a nerve somewhere. Interestingly, there were very few people who knew. Cheryl considered this for a moment. "You're right. I need to tell someone. Could you follow me back to security for the report? I hate to hold you up."

Jerry replied, "Ma'am, after all the things you've done for this hospital, I would consider it an honor to escort you."

She responded, "You're most kind."

Willie was on duty in the security office. When she walked in with Jerry, he popped to attention.

Cheryl took a reassuring tone with him. "Willie, I need to file a report." She patted Jerry on the arm. "Thank you. I'll be fine from here. You go home and look after Melody. How's she doing?"

He replied, "She's good. She's starting to open up a bit more each day. I can't tell you how much it means to me to have my daughter back whole again, ma'am."

Cheryl patted him on the arm. "You're a good daddy, Jerry. Now go home and be with your little girl."

Jerry replied, "Thank you, ma'am," and left the room.

Cheryl turned to Willie. Without pretense, she began, "I was walking to my car when a man pinned me against my car—"

Willie interrupted her. "Dr. B, we should call the police on this."

Cheryl gave him a reassuring smile. "I'm fine, Willie. If we can document the incident, that will be sufficient."

Thirty minutes later, Willie finished his draft of the report. "I'll walk you to your car, ma'am."

Cheryl responded, "That would be appreciated."

****

Amit was having his apartment painted. Cheryl had subtly suggested that he move in with her during the work. Their relationship in college had been comfortable, casual even. They had kept in touch since med school, but she realized that her feelings for Amit ran deeper than she cared to admit.

When she arrived at her apartment, the smell of curry chicken wafted from the kitchen. Amit was happily preparing a traditional recipe with rice. He was absolutely the most unique Indian she had ever met. Most men from Southern India did not cook. He seemed quite happy in the kitchen. She was happy to have him here. The table was set for two, with Max circling Amit's legs. She thought to herself, *it takes a skilled cook to work around pets. I wish I could cook something that didn't come with microwave instructions.*

She greeted him, "So what's for dinner?"

He looked at her. "Chicken curry. On the plantation, my mother always cooked. When I was small, I would stay with her in the kitchen. Fighting spiders and cobras in the fields did not interest me in the least. So she taught me to cook. She was a doctor

125

herself before she married my father. I guess that is what made me want to come to America to study medicine."

Cheryl probed, "Do they know you're dating American women?"

Amit laughed. "Of course. Mothers know everything. She is fine with it. My younger brother will inherit the plantation. Which is fine with me. He loves it."

There was concern in Cheryl's eyes. "And your father? How does he feel about this?"

Amit poured white wine into two glasses on the kitchen counter. "He will be fine. My mother will convince him that it is for the best."

She pulled out a stool and sat. "I hate to change the subject, but there's something I need to tell you."

There was something in her eyes that made him pause. He tried to lighten the mood. "If it's the chicken, I can fix you pork next time…"

The surge of emotion washed over her. She tried to hold back the tears. "It's not you. It's not us. It's…well…I was assaulted tonight." Saying it out loud to Amit made the reality stick. Tears welled up in her eyes. She covered her face with her hands.

The blood drained from Amit's face and he dropped his wine glass to the floor. It shattered, spilling wine all over the floor. He paid it no attention as he moved to her side. He pulled her close to him. She buried her face in his chest, muffling the sobs that racked her body. Gently he probed, "Do we need to go back to the hospital?"

She placed her hand on his arm and reassured him, "I'm fine. He pinned me to the car, but nothing else.

Jerry came up behind us and saved me."

Amit led her to the sofa. Gently he held her hand. His hands were warm and strong. Cheryl wiped the tears from her eyes. "Amit, this is important. I need you to be honest with me. Have you told anyone that I'm going to the FBI office Thursday?"

He shook his head. "No. Absolutely not. I know very few people at the hospital and can't say who I can trust yet. So no, your secret is safe with me."

She believed him. "I know. But I had to ask. Someone seems to know about it. And they're trying to stop it. Let's eat while it's hot, and I'll call Dwight."

The chicken dish was incredible, but Cheryl couldn't help but pick at it. The more she thought about what happened, the madder she got. Finally, she gave up. "Save this for me. I'll reheat it later." She stood and stalked to the bedroom with her phone.

The phone rang only twice. The voice on the other end was crisp and professional. "Dwight Ironsides."

"Hi, Dwight. It's Cheryl. I need to tell you something."

Dwight didn't interrupt as Cheryl spoke almost without breathing. When she had finished, he responded, "Cheryl, I can assure you, I have not told anyone. This is very concerning. Is it possible someone overheard you?"

She considered the question for a moment. "I don't believe so. I haven't confided in anyone at the hospital. George is the only person I've discussed it with. I would think that if he wanted to stop me, he would have said so."

Dwight replied, "You would think so. But we don't know who he told. Let's play it safe. I will follow you to work tomorrow, and you need to bring in some extra security. Can you do that?"

"I'll do what I can."

Dwight could detect the uncertainty in her voice. "Better yet, I have some friends that can help out in cases like this. Are you in a safe place tonight?"

"I'm fine. My boyfriend is here with me. Are you sure this is necessary?"

"Cheryl, if this person was brazen enough to attack you in the open, he is capable of far more. I think we need to escalate this now—you can't predict what people will do. Does that make sense?"

She saw his point. This was his line of work. "Okay. I'll wait for you in the morning."

"Very good. I'll be there at seven thirty sharp."

"Uh, well, okay. That seems early."

"It is. Things will be a little different over the next couple of days, but it will all work out. Trust me."

"All right. I'll see you then."

She hung up the phone. What had she gotten herself into?

****

Amit kissed her goodbye the next morning as she climbed into Dwight's SUV. It was big, black with tinted windows. It looked like something from a spy movie.

Dwight was cordial, but all business. "Put your case in the floorboard of the back seat."

She did as she was told. Dwight was not much for conversation; he scanned the area around them as he drove. In a short while they pulled up to the front of the hospital where a man in a blue blazer waited in a tan car that looked like an old police cruiser. With the window down, she could see his breath in the air in the chill of the morning. This surprised Cheryl. As Dwight pulled up, the man exited the vehicle. He was well over six feet, and she could tell he was muscular even with the heavy winter clothing. A scar on his cheek was not deep, but noticeable. His dark skin seemed to glow in the morning sun.

Dwight got out with her. "Cheryl, this is Harry. He will be with you today. If there is any trouble, Harry will deal with it. All right?"

Her eyes were wide. "Sure." She didn't know how to feel. She was relieved that she had someone to watch over her, but she seemed a bit intimidated that she had a man assigned to protect her. As she moved through the front door, Marge waited for her, smiling.

She whipped up a quick cover story for Harry. "Hi, Marge. This is Harry. He's an interior decorator. I'm going to get his help with bringing my office up to date."

Marge's eyes grew wide. "Well, okay. Whatever you say, Dr. B. Have fun with that."

Harry's face was stoic. He didn't say a word the entire trip to her office. And everywhere that Cheryl went, Harry was sure to follow.

Her mind was a blur as she went through the day. She could barely concentrate on the work at hand. She met with Ray while Harry waited outside the office. This was not working. She cut the day short. It seemed that her new friend had drawn unnecessary attention. It was just as well. Tomorrow would be a long day for her.

Harry walked her back downstairs to where Dwight was waiting with the SUV. He opened the door for her.

As she entered, before he shut the door, Harry spoke for the first time all day. "You know, Dr. Blumenthal, I wanted to be an interior designer, but I have no sense of color."

Cheryl cocked an eyebrow. "Really?"

He grinned. "No, Doctor. I'm just kidding. Good luck tomorrow." Harry shut the door.

Dwight drove her home without speaking. This could not end soon enough for her.

****

There was a bite in the air that left Cheryl with a chill that stuck to her like glue. It was several minutes in the warmth of the SUV before she stopped shaking. Dwight looked straight forward as he spoke. "Do you have all the documentation you need?"

Cheryl did the same. "Yes. Plus, I brought supporting documentation from the bank." She pulled out a folder and began to review the documents. They had not left her sight since the incident two days ago. The accounting report from Blankenship and Rice contained unequivocal evidence in support of the conclusions Kelly had made.

Raleigh traffic stood at a standstill. It was the usual morning rush. Dwight took a side road and almost magically transported them to Capital Boulevard and into a parking deck where he conveniently had an access badge to enter. For a private investigator from a small town, he had impressive resources. The receptionist buzzed them into the lobby. Her desk was an orderly beehive. Her navy suit was neatly pressed, and her back was ramrod straight even seated behind the desk.

Dwight spoke before Cheryl could open her mouth.

"Hi, Kathy. We're here to see Luke Davis." Cheryl gave Dwight a sideways glance. Not only did he have a pass to the parking garage, he knew the receptionist on a first name basis.

Agent Davis wasted no time in coming out to see them. He was a tall man, almost as tall as Harry. But he was much thinner. He greeted them warmly. His soft Southern drawl was smooth like aged bourbon. He shook Cheryl's hand as he greeted her. His grip was strong but not aggressively so. He led them to a small corner office. The office was simple and had no personal items other than his FBI National Academy Certification, and an MBA from Auburn University in Accountancy. Those two pieces of paper alone gave her confidence that she was talking to the right person.

They sat at a small round table with three chairs. Cheryl began to explain, and Agent Davis took notes as she spoke. She was transparent about her suspension and subsequent appointment as the hospital director. She relayed the concern over the hospital's finances and the call for an audit by a third party.

Agent Davis stopped her. "And who is your controller or hospital chief accountant?"

Cheryl took a breath. "Delores Smythe." She continued with everything she could remember.

When she finished, Agent Davis asked, "Do you have any documentation with you?"

Cheryl nodded and placed the portfolio in front of her. She began to remove the folders of paper and place them in neat rows facing Agent Davis.

He looked over the files and looked up at Cheryl. "It will take some time to go through this; once I do, I cannot turn a blind eye to anything I find."

Cheryl had a serious look in her eye. "I started this because something is wrong and there are a lot of people depending on me to make this right. I'm in this for the long haul."

Agent Davis did not waver. "I appreciate your candor. If there is deliberate criminal activity, people will be prosecuted."

She replied, "I understand."

For the next three hours, Agent Davis went through every piece of paper. He took notes, asked questions, and finally sat back. Dwight and Cheryl looked up.

"Well, ma'am, it is clear to me that there are some significant irregularities. I can't say exactly what; I'll have to obtain more data from the bank. We may have to obtain a court order for documents for that. It's evident that a substantial amount of money was borrowed to secure funds to add onto the hospital, but there is no evidence of construction or even plans for construction. No invoices from architects, city planners, or permits are available. It's a good thing you brought this to our attention, because if this were to have gone on much longer, you might have been implicated."

Cheryl's breath drew in sharply.

Agent Davis reassured her. "The paper trail began before you were hired by the hospital. It seems unlikely that you could be implicated at this point. You've been left holding the proverbial bag, so to speak."

Cheryl leaned forward. "Can we figure out who orchestrated this?"

Agent Davis replied, "Oh yes, ma'am. That's what I do for a living. I'm a forensic accountant."

Cheryl looked at Dwight, who smiled for the first time of the day. "As I said, Cheryl, I know some people that can help you."

She sat back. "So what are our next steps?"

Agent Davis threaded his fingers together. "I'll have to obtain a subpoena for bank records and scrub through the original documents to verify. I might have to investigate some of the bank officers to rule out collusion outside of the hospital. This could take a while."

Cheryl got a little frustrated. "What do I do in the meantime? I've been threatened because of this."

Agent Davis looked at Dwight. "Is this true?"

Dwight responded, "She was assaulted two nights ago. As she gets closer, people are getting more nervous."

Agent Davis took more notes. "Generally, we don't provide protective custody for embezzlement cases like this. But I will check with our section chief."

Dwight spoke up. "We can provide some protective custody, but it's costing the hospital and they're obviously struggling as it is."

Cheryl replied, "If we go much deeper in debt, I will have trouble making payroll."

Agent Davis responded, "That is a problem. Let's talk to the deputy director after lunch. Meet me back her at two o'clock. I'll see what I can arrange."

Dwight grinned at Cheryl. "Come on, I'll take you to lunch."

****

The restaurant was small but neat; wood floors and brick walls set the stage for an eclectic array of vintage enamel kitchen tables and old office chairs. The Sweet Southern Home Cookin' restaurant was off the beaten track, but business was steady and faithful. The menu was typical—fried chicken or catfish, okra, sweet potatoes, as well as fried green tomatoes and collards. The tea was sweet and the music lively. Their server was Grace. Her Jamaican accent was lovely, and her brown eyes glowed with life. It was the break Cheryl needed. She never asked about refills on tea, as their glasses seemed to magically refill when Grace was around. It was a comfortable place. Far removed from the intensity of the morning.

Cheryl looked worried. "Dwight, how long will the investigation take? I'm not complaining, and I am serious about the principle of the matter, but I can't stay under house protection and run a hospital."

Dwight replied, "I understand. We will have to get a bit creative, but it will all work out."

Cheryl looked at him seriously. "You promise?"

Dwight responded, "I promise."

****

Deputy Director Terrance Hall had piercing hazel eyes and silver hair at the temples. The silver stood out in stark contrast to the jet-black hair on the rest of his head. He was a seasoned agent with little capacity for nonsense. This was not to say that he lacked empathy. The section was lucky to have him. Different sections called him for guidance routinely.

Agent Davis introduced Cheryl to the senior director but did not introduce Dwight. Cheryl thought it somewhat curious but did not try to read a lot into it. Director Hall motioned for Cheryl to sit. The director's office was more spacious than Agent Davis' tight quarters. Pictures lined the walls with former directors and presidents. He was a man who was well connected.

The director began carefully. "Dr. Blumenthal,

Agent Davis has disclosed the findings from your internal investigation. The FBI would like to thank you for bringing this forward, and we are sensitive to your position with the county's health system. I need to understand from you, do you feel that you are being threatened because of your investigation?"

Cheryl measured her response. She was a fast learner. "I believe that I have uncovered a plot that threatens the solvency of my institution. I also believe that the people who have orchestrated this plan are capable of doing whatever is necessary to make me stop the inquiry. It appears they are willing and able to escalate threats to violence according to how far I'm willing to go. So, my answer, sir, is yes. I feel threatened."

The director nodded. "Thank you for your candor, Dr. Blumenthal. I will discuss our strategy to escalate this case with Agent Davis. He will communicate to you within the next forty-eight hours. Is that satisfactory?"

Cheryl replied, "Thank you, sir. We are the primary intake for low-income families in the county. It would jeopardize the welfare of hundreds of people if we could not operate."

The director stood. "Thank you for all of your efforts, Dr. Blumenthal. Wise Regional is lucky to have a director like you."

His statement surprised her. She had never seen herself in that light. Director Hall came around the desk and shook her hand. "We'll sort this out. I promise." For the first time since they had met, the director turned to Dwight. "It's a pleasure seeing you again, Dwight. I take it you'll care for the good doctor for a couple of days?"

Dwight responded, "I promise, sir."

The director turned to Agent Davis. "Luke, stay behind for a minute. I want to review your current case load and see what we can do to re-prioritize what you're working on."

Agent Davis replied, "Yes, sir," and remained as Cheryl and Dwight left the office. Within minutes, they were on the road.

Cheryl could not contain herself. "Dwight, I don't mean to pry, but you seem to know an awful lot about this place."

Dwight didn't turn his head. "I was a field agent here for ten years. I left on disability after taking a gunshot to the chest on a drug bust in Charlotte. I dove between the shooter and another field agent. He was a rookie agent. It was his first field assignment. I wasn't about to let him die on his first bust."

It all made sense. Dwight was a real hero. "So, let me guess, the agent's life you saved was Agent Davis."

Dwight turned toward her. "Heck, no. The kid's name was Bruce. He didn't last more than a year with the Bureau. He was book smart but didn't have any street sense. We train for months at Quantico, but none of that compares to the real thing. Some agents just aren't cut out for fieldwork. Bruce is practicing law in Maryland. I get a Christmas card from him every year. Pictures of his kids, that sort of thing."

Cheryl took it all in. "So what is your opinion of what will happen next?"

Dwight was silent for a moment. "Well, if no one at the hospital knows, and you and I haven't told anyone, that only leaves one person who could have leaked this: George."

Cheryl considered this for a moment. "That doesn't make sense. He could have easily told me not to involve the authorities. He is very rich. He could have made up the difference at the hospital with petty cash."

Dwight shrugged. "One lesson I learned years ago—don't let appearances fool you. What people say and how they act in public can be a false front. I investigated a lot of cases in my day. You would be amazed at how many people own two million dollar homes with no furniture in them."

Cheryl snorted. "Really?"

Dwight responded, "Really!"

A light rain had begun misting the air, making the roads wet. They crossed the county line with rain falling steadily. Traffic was light as they cruised down the narrow highway. The straightaway was long with only a dump truck coming toward them in the opposite lane. At one hundred feet, the truck swerved into their lane. Everything seemed to slow down. Cheryl could see the grill of the truck getting larger. Dwight swerved into the opposite lane as the truck struck the rear quarter panel of the SUV. The SUV spun out of control rolling through the pasture. Cheryl screamed as it rolled. She could barely make out anything from the maelstrom of debris flying in the SUV. As it struck the ground, blackness engulfed her, and all was quiet.

Chapter 14

Everything was surreal. Lights surrounded her. Blue, red, yellow. Garbled sounds filtered through. She could hear people shouting, but she couldn't tell what they were saying. An upside-down face appeared in front of her.

Through the din, it sounded like, "You're okay. We're going to…"

She lost the voice in a haze of distortion. The crushing pressure to her shoulder was unyielding. She could taste blood in her mouth. Suddenly she was surrounded by white light. She could not move her head. And then, blissful relief of her body as she was released from the pressure. She felt weightless but confined. A light rain fell on her face; it felt good against her skin. A face appeared again. This time it was right side up. He was a young man. He had a round boyish face and strawberry blond curls.

He spoke. "Ma'am, my name is David. You've been in an automobile accident. We're taking you to the hospital. Can you tell me your name?"

Cheryl blinked. She focused on what David said. She blinked again. "Cheryl, Cheryl Blumenthal. Take me to Wise Regional."

David responded, "Ma'am, that is another ten minutes away. We can have you at County General is less time."

Her head cleared a bit. "Take me to Wise, David."

David replied, "Yes, ma'am."

Cheryl stopped him. "David?"

David responded, "Yes, ma'am?"

Cheryl asked, "How is the driver?"

David looked away for a moment, then back at Cheryl. "He's unconscious. Vitals are good. They're removing him from the vehicle. Like you, ma'am, he is upside down. The vehicle is overturned."

Exhausted, she lay back. The smell of gasoline made her nauseous. Her eyes opened wide. "David!"

David replied, "Here, ma'am."

Cheryl stated, "I smell gasoline."

David responded, "Yes, ma'am, the fire department is foaming the vehicle to prevent the fire, but we've got to get you out of here. It's a very dangerous situation."

The stretcher bounced along the rough terrain. As she moved, she felt the mask being attached to her face and the cold dryness of oxygen flooded the mask. The gurney jostled as it banged into the back of the ambulance. Finally, she had stopped moving. The prick in her arm and the slight burn of IV fluid signaled the start of a drip. The door slammed shut to the ambulance, and it began to move forward jostling her around. They were no more than a minute down the road when the sound of an explosion could be heard.

Cheryl gasped. "Dwight…"

David heard her. His face appeared over her. "Your friend is okay. He was out of the vehicle and away before the vehicle blew, ma'am."

She closed her eyes. She tried not to cry, but the tears streamed out of the corners of her eyes. *This is all my fault*, was all she could think. The hiss of the oxygen mask covered the sounds of her quiet weeping.

****

Familiar faces surrounded her as the doors opened and the gurney was unloaded at the ER. Louise appeared over her, checking her pupils. Her voice seemed far away as she said, "Honey, I've got you now. There ain't nothing going to happen to you while I'm here." Her brown eyes could not lie. She was worried.

Boomer was beside her shouting orders to the ER team. Amit and Darlene moved in. Amit's face was taut, his lips thin. He forced a reassuring smile to hide his worry. Cheryl held out her hand. He took it gently.

His voice was barely a whisper. "You're going to be okay."

They rolled her into the examining room.

****

When Cheryl awoke, every muscle felt like it was on fire. She could move, but it hurt to blink. She was alive, that was all that mattered. Amit was in the chair beside her asleep. Louise was checking her vitals. "How you feelin', honey?"

Cheryl replied, "Like I've got hit by a Mack truck. Oh wait, I did." Cheryl managed a faint smile.

Louise inspected her IV and looked over her glasses at Cheryl. "Child, the Lord was looking after you. Another two feet and we would have been singing hymns for you."

Cheryl's eyes grew wide. "Dwight! How is Dwight?"

Louise patted her hand gently. "Like you. Sore and lucky."

Cheryl asked Louise, "Is he here? Can I speak with him?"

Louise flicked the IV bag, "Two doors down in 306. He's talking to the state man right now. I suspect you might get a visit next."

Cheryl scanned herself. "What kind of state man?"

Louise gave her a sly look. "Why, North Carolina's finest, honey, the State Highway Patrol, of course."

Cheryl nodded. Even that hurt. Louise leaned close. "You take care, honey. I'll be back to check on you in a bit." She leaned over, gave her a quick kiss on the forehead, and walked out. Amit rose and took Cheryl's hand. With his free hand, he stroked her hair. No one had stroked her hair like that since her mother. It was comforting.

He was more composed than the night before. "How are you feeling?"

She lied. "Not bad, all things considered."

He looked deeply into her eyes. "I realized something last night. Something that I was not ready for."

Cheryl responded, "What was that?"

Amit took a deep breath. "I love you. When you came into the hospital from the accident last night, all I could think of was I could not go on without you. I hope you do not feel less of me for my weakness."

Tears welled in Cheryl's eyes. "Love is not weakness; it is the truest test of strength. And yes, Amit, I love you too."

He leaned over and kissed her gently on the lips. As they parted, she said, "Oww."

She could see the anguish in his eyes; she placed her fingers on his face and smiled. "It's all good."

There was a knock on the door. Cheryl responded, "Come in."

The trooper was tall. His gray uniform was tight and crisp. His dark skin made it hard to see his face in the glare of fluorescent light over her bed. His voice was deep. "Dr. Blumenthal?"

Cheryl responded, "I'm Dr. Blumenthal."

The trooper continued, "Ma'am, I am State Highway Patrolman Youngblood. I'm investigating the traffic accident that occurred last evening with a black SUV driven by a Mr. Dwight Ironsides. Were you a passenger in that vehicle at the time of the accident?"

She felt like she was in a courtroom not a hospital bed. "I was."

The trooper asked, "Dr. Blumenthal, may I take a statement from you at this time? If it is not a good time, I can come back later."

Cheryl nodded. "Now is fine." She looked at Amit. "Could you get me some ice water, please?" Amit stood and left the room.

The trooper pulled a small notebook from his pocket. "Ma'am, in your own words, can you tell me what happened?"

Cheryl began with the two-lane road the accident occurred on and then recounted in as much detail as she could.

When she had finished, the trooper asked, "Ma'am, was there any alcohol consumed by the driver before the accident?"

Cheryl was surprised by the question. "No. Certainly not."

The trooper pressed. "Is there anything you can tell me about your relationship with Mr. Ironsides?"

Again, surprised by the question. "Mr. Ironsides is currently employed by me."

The trooper took notes, "In what capacity, ma'am?"

Cheryl raised the bed up so she could look at the trooper more directly. She asked, "May I speak off the record?"

The trooper closed the pad. "Of course, ma'am."

"Trooper Youngblood, Mr. Ironsides and I are in the middle of an investigation that is sensitive to the hospital. We were returning from a meeting with the FBI in Raleigh to provide evidence to their agents in order to escalate the investigation into the proper hands. The reason Mr. Ironsides was driving was because I was assaulted recently to attempt to frighten me away from pursuing this investigation. Mr. Ironsides was trying to protect me."

The trooper replied, "I know, ma'am. I just needed you to say that."

Cheryl looked confused. "Why, for heaven's sake?"

The trooper continued, "Because Mr. Ironsides' duty is to protect client privilege. Ma'am, he could not tell me any of this himself. You were very nearly killed last night. I worked the accident scene. Based on my assessment of the situation, if anyone else had been driving that vehicle this would have been a fatality investigation. He turned into the vehicle that collided with you at exactly the right moment. You owe your life to Mr. Ironsides."

Cheryl realized the gravity of the situation. "It also means it's possible that it was deliberate."

Trooper Youngblood replied, "Yes, ma'am. The driver of the second vehicle did not stop. It may have been an accident. It seems very suspicious. Can you advise me of the person you worked with at the FBI?"

Cheryl replied, "Agent Luke Davis."

The trooper reopened his notebook and wrote down Agent Davis's name. "Would it be acceptable for me to contact Agent Davis to confirm you story?"

Cheryl replied, her mind racing with other things. "Yes, of course. Just leave that detail out of any reports that might be accessible to others."

The trooper scribbled more of her personal information. As he left the room Cheryl rang the nurse's call bell. Louise poked her head in the door. "Whatcha need, hun?"

Cheryl didn't blink. "Some underwear; I need to go see Dwight."

Louise gave her a stern look, "Little early for you to get out of bed, isn't it?"

Cheryl swung her legs over the side of the bed. "Louise, we don't have time for this."

The matronly nurse helped her with her skivvies and called for a wheelchair.

****

Hazel Ironsides sat beside her husband. Dwight was sitting up eating scrambled eggs with ketchup and bacon. When Cheryl rolled into the room, he stopped eating and placed his fork carefully on the plate. "Cheryl, I'm sorry. I thought I was going to miss—"

She raised her hand and cut him off. "Dwight, stop. None of this is your fault. I've dragged you into something that nearly got us killed. I think we need to abandon the investigation. I can't risk getting someone killed over a financial discrepancy."

Dwight took a sip of coffee. "Cheryl, you can't blame yourself for this. And I don't think we can simply walk away from it. We have passed the point of no return. As for me"—he patted Hazel's hand—"this is my life. This is the third time the Lord has kept me alive. And I can't help but think there's a reason for it. Before I went in the FBI, I was in military intelligence in Afghanistan. We were trying to pinpoint the leader of a Taliban cell that was orchestrating ambushes on patrols. We were close to finding him. The next morning, I was headed back to my rack, and there was this boy standing in front of my Chu. When he saw me, he started walking away. He wasn't in a hurry. But he kept looking back at me, so I followed him. When I was about fifty feet from my Chu, it blew up. I'll never know if that kid was sent to kill me or save me. All I knew was I didn't stop until I got the T-man. Cheryl, sometimes these things are awful and scary as hell, but you can't quit. You've just got to see it through. This wasn't your fault. Bad people did this. And if bad people are willing to kill you to stop this, then they need to be stopped, because they'll hurt other people too."

There was no arguing with his logic. It occurred to her that this was more than fraud. It was more than running a hospital. It was about saving the hospital—not just the building, but the people in it. For the first time, she could see the enormity of it. For the first time, she could feel the weight she was carrying. Just as she thought she might crumble into a pit from which she would not return, she felt Louise's hand on her shoulder.

In a soft Southern drawl, she said, "Honey, I'm with you to the end, no matter what you do. I believe in you. So do a lot of other people around here."

Dwight and Hazel nodded in agreement.

In the quiet of the moment, the tide turned. Resolve lifted her out of the void. She was meant to do this. This was her time; every test in her life had readied her for this. It was time to test her mettle. She looked up at Louise first, then at Dwight. "Then we see this through."

Chapter 15

Cheryl was released from the hospital the next day. She moved slowly through the lobby. She spied Dalton straightening up magazines while Marge gave directions to an elderly couple on how the find the ICU waiting room.

Dalton made his way toward her. "Dr. B, can we talk?"

She responded, "Of course, Dalton. Why don't you walk with me to my office?"

Dalton looked behind Cheryl and noticed the large dark man behind them. He swallowed nervously and whispered, "Dr. B, I think there's a man following you."

Cheryl looked back at Harry. She placed her arm on his shoulder. "He's my interior decorator. He's going to turn my office from drab to fab." She winked at Dalton. Dalton stole another glance at Harry.

Cheryl asked Dalton, "So what do we need to talk about? Is this a doctor kind of question or something else?"

Dalton looked up at her with deeply serious eyes. "It's something else. I need to talk to you in private, please. And I don't need to talk about my puberty, if that's what you're thinking."

She laughed and changed the subject. "So, how is your piano playing coming?"

He flexed his hand at her. "Really good. I'm almost at one hundred percent. I was worried when the cast came off, because I could barely move my fingers, but that nice lady in physical therapy showed me exercises on how to move my hand to make it loosen up. It feels almost as good as new."

Cheryl replied, "That's the great thing about being young. You heal fast. I feel very fortunate that I was able to help you."

Dalton's brow furrowed. "I'm sorry you got in trouble."

Cheryl squeezed him tight against her. She didn't know that Dalton knew she had been put on administrative leave. "Sometimes things like that happen. We take chances, and they don't turn out the way we planned. But we learn from those events, and those difficult times prepare us for bigger things in the future."

They arrived at her office. There were fresh pink and white roses on her desk. The card was signed simply *Love, A*. Amit was really beginning to grow on her.

She closed the door behind Dalton and motioned him to a chair. She sat beside him versus going around the desk. "So, what's up?"

He took a deep breath. "I was on the third floor straightening out the waiting room. There was a man in there. He made me nervous. I heard him say, 'Yeah, she's alive. I'll take care of that soon enough.' I kind of thought he might be talking about you. When he saw me, he turned away and said something I couldn't hear and then walked out of the room. Dr. B, I've never been afraid in the hospital before, but that man made me scared."

Cheryl looked Dalton in the eye and placed her hands on his. "Dalton, what you've said is very important. Can you tell me what the man looked like?"

Dalton nodded. She rose painfully from the chair and moved to the door. She peeped out. "Harry, I need you for a minute."

Harry rose and moved into the office. "Yes, ma'am?"

She rested her hand on Harry's arm. "Do we know any good sketch artists?"

Harry replied, "Yes, ma'am, we do. Some of the best."

She responded, "Well, Dalton here has something he needs to share with us. Could you arrange something for us?"

Harry removed his phone and walked out of the office.

Dalton looked up at Cheryl. "Dr. B, did I say something wrong?"

She smiled down at him. "No, Dalton. You might have just helped us more than you know. We're going to ask for some help from people who can draw the person you saw. It won't take long. Is that okay?"

He grinned. "Sure. It's a teacher's workday, so I don't have anywhere to be. I think I do need to let Mom know where I am though, if that's okay."

Cheryl replied, "Of course. Use the phone on my desk to call her."

His eyes went wide. "Wow, I can use your phone?"

She replied, almost amused at the question, "Of course, it's just a phone."

His eyes sparkled. "Can I sit in your chair?"

She gave him as fake a stern look she could muster. "I don't know about that."

Grinning, he pleaded, "Aww, come one."

She laughed. "Yes, you can use my chair."

He wiggled himself into the seat, picked up the phone, and dialed reception. After a brief pause, "Hey Mom, guess where I'm at?"

****

It took almost an hour and a half for the sketch artist to arrive. Tanya was a plump, middle-aged woman with deep brown eyes and a cheery face. She went to work with Dalton at the table in Cheryl's office. After an hour, they were finishing up. Dalton looked at the picture carefully. He pointed to the image of a tattoo on the man's neck. "There were drops coming off the fangs, there."

Cheryl stared at the sketch. She knew the face from somewhere. The tattoo was unmistakable.

****

She struggled against the seat belt which felt like it was cutting her in two. It was unmovable. Her legs were trapped by some object in the floorboard; it was red, with a white cross. She realized that it was a medical jump kit for field use. How ironic, she was trapped by a rescue kit. She could move her head. She looked to the right, a shadow caught her eye. It moved slowly toward her. Thank God, someone is here to save me. The face became clearer, thin watery blue eyes, stringy brown hair, a row of jagged teeth leering at her from the murk. The cobra tattoo seemed to move on his neck. Her blood ran cold. She struggled against the seatbelt which seemed to grow tighter. The panic began to rise in her. Cobra man leered at her with his broken smile. She heard the click, and then cobra man raised the knife. He toyed with the blade. He stroked it with a lover's touch. She tried to scream, but she had no voice. He edged closer. The chill of the fog seethed around her, engulfing her. His voice hissed like a snake. "Told you to stay away from them Feds. You just wouldn't listen, would you?"

Cobra man stepped closer, sliding his finger along the blade; his finger bled. His tongue came out and licked the blood from his finger. His tongue was forked like that of a snake; it quivered at the taste of blood. Fascinated and horrified, she watched until the tongue returned to his mouth. She looked into his eyes. They were slits. With all of her strength, she screamed...

The room was black around her. Amit turned on the lamp. She was sitting straight up in the bed, her hair matted with sweat. She fell sobbing into his arms. He held her tight and caressed her hair. The shock of the dream wore off.

She gasped out in ragged sentences, "—and I couldn't get free...and he cut his finger on purpose...and he had a snake's tongue..." She stopped in mid-sentence and pulled back. "Oh, my Lord, I know who he is."

Amit stared at her. "Who is it that you know?"

Cheryl replied, "The man from my dream. It was the same person Dalton saw. It was the same person I saw at the Wise estate at the party."

Amit looked concerned. "We must report this."

Cheryl shook her head. "I can't go to the police with a dream. But I know where I saw him. I'll call Dwight in the morning."

She tossed and turned the rest of the night. The

nightmare weighed on her heavily. Tired of lying awake, she slipped from the bed and showered. The hot water washed away the fog and soothed some of the lingering tightness. She looked at the clock periodically. It seemed to be taking forever for the time to pass. At seven a.m., she could wait no longer. She dialed Dwight. When he answered, she couldn't contain it any longer. "I know who the man with the cobra tattoo is!"

Dwight was silent for a second. "Okay. And what is the significance of this person?"

She was stunned. "Didn't Harry tell you?"

Dwight's response was slow and halting. "He stated that one of the boys at the hospital saw a man with a tattoo on the side of his neck. The man had acted suspiciously when they were in the ward."

It all seemed so obvious to Cheryl. She couldn't understand why Dwight couldn't see it. "Precisely! He is the same man I saw at the Christmas party at the Wise house. I think he might be the man that assaulted me in the parking lot. It's all connected."

Dwight was silent for a moment. "Cheryl, all you have is circumstantial. We need proof."

She was frustrated. "Fine. If we need proof, I'll get proof."

Dwight tried to soothe her. "Hold on. Don't charge off mad. Let's work out a plan for this, okay?"

She held her frustration in check. "Okay. So, what are our next steps?"

The phone was silent for a second before Dwight replied. "We'll have to obtain his name and birthdate, so we can run a background check on him. We can't go in too aggressively, or we'll tip our hand that we suspect him. He could run or destroy evidence. I have an idea that might work. Be patient, all right?"

Cheryl sighed. "I'll be patient."

The day was one long meeting after another. By noon, she was beginning to wonder if there was any end to the issues the staff needed her help on. Horace appeared in her doorway and tapped on the framework. He was a welcome change to the day. Cheryl looked up. "Hi, Horace. How are you?"

He responded, "I know you're busy, but do you have a free moment to walk with me?"

She stared at the pile of papers in front of her. They would be there waiting for her when she returned. She eased around the desk. The old man extended his hand and took hers. It was an old custom, and one of endearment. They walked down the hall, hand in hand.

Horace spoke as they meandered across the polished floor. "You know when you called me to help with the children, I was a little nervous at first. It's been years since I've watched little ones."

Cheryl felt a sudden pang of guilt. She had been so wrapped up in the financial issues of the hospital she had all but forgotten about the Childcare Center. She stopped. "Oh Horace, I am so sorry!"

He cut her off. "No. This isn't about that. I need you to understand, you've helped me." He dropped her hand and put his arm around her shoulder urging her forward. "For years, I've sat around on that farm with nothing to do but work on that house. Barley's a good companion, but I don't have a lot of contact with people. This place gave me a fresh perspective on life. These are good kids. I've enjoyed every minute of my time here, and I'd like to keep on if the good Lord allows. Kids make you young."

Cheryl smiled as she nodded. As they entered the hall to the Childcare Center, it was noticeably different. The lights had been replaced, and the hall was painted a pale blue with flowers lining the chair rail along the wall. Butterflies adorned the walls sporadically, giving the hall a glow. She smelled the food before she saw it. A spread was laid out in the room where there were almost twice as many children as before and their parents. James and Marge stood side by side smiling at her.

She looked at Horace. "How is this possible? We don't have the budget to hire painters."

He patted her on the back. "The same way most things get done, by people rolling up their sleeves and pitching in. All the parents and the kids helped. We decided to have a potluck lunch."

It was the most astounding transformation she had ever seen. The room was alive. The children were happy; the parents beamed.

Boomer sat in the corner making balloon animals. A talent she was unaware of. Darlene was face painting. Cheryl realized this is what she was fighting for. The bricks and mortar were irrelevant. There was positive energy in the air. It was palpable. She would not rest until her new family was safe.

She felt her phone vibrate. The call was from Dwight. She stepped into the hallway. "Yes, Dwight?"

Dwight almost sounded excited as he said, "Cheryl, it appears that your intuition paid off. We need to talk in person."

Chapter 16

Cheryl couldn't decide if she was thrilled that she had figured out a key piece of the puzzle or if she was going to throw up. At this point both seemed plausible. Harry drove the black SUV out of town. It looked almost identical to the first one she and Dwight had been in when they collided with the dump truck. Dwight must have cornered the market on aftermarket government package SUVs. They stopped at Pancake Palace near Green Lake. It was a fine establishment twenty years ago before the interstate took away most of the business. Now, it was a place that the locals went to for cheap food. Dwight sat in a booth with Agent Davis, nursing a cup of coffee. Their waitress, Eloise, sauntered up to the table in purple bedroom slippers. She turned her head and coughed raggedly. Cheryl wondered if she was related to the waitress at Dot's Diner.

Eloise cordially asked, "What'll it be, sweetheart?"

Cheryl considered her options quickly. "Anything diet and dark."

Eloise looked at Harry. "And you, hun?"

Harry grinned, showing pearly white teeth. "Coffee, cream, and sugar." Without a word, Eloise began her slow trek back to the counter.

Cheryl looked across the table at Dwight. "So, what did we learn?"

155

"It seems our tattooed friend is one Bernard Jacob 'Skeeter' Ross, born in Georgia. Suspected in a capital case in Georgia, but they didn't have enough evidence to hold him. He lives here with his uncle who owns a small grading business. He is the groundskeeper at the Wise estate. Why they would hire a man like that I have no idea. He's a handyman. He does odd jobs as needed. He drives a green 1986 Datsun truck. He's kept off the local radar to date, but he was quite the rabble-rouser when he lived in Georgia."

Cheryl looked puzzled. "So he works for George Wise. That doesn't make any sense. Why would he hire a thug and risk scrutiny by the FBI? Do we know if George is in any financial trouble?"

Dwight replied, "George's balance sheets are numerous and on file with the SEC. His net worth is not a façade. He really could bail the hospital out in short order and never notice and never blink. But George isn't the only person at the estate. His son lives there as well. If the staff was in collusion to embezzle money, his son Albert would be in the middle of it. All we have now is theories. What we need is direct evidence."

Cheryl squinted one eye at Dwight. "And how are you proposing we get direct evidence?"

Dwight flashed a devilish smile. "I have a plan."

****

A frigid north wind whisked dried oak leaves across the imported red terracotta tiles. Purple cabbage and pansies bravely endured the late winter chill. Cheryl rang the doorbell at the massive Wise estate. She was surprised when Charlotte Wise greeted her at the door with a whiskey tumbler in her hand.

Charlotte grinned broadly. "Why, Cheryl, what a

lovely surprise! Please come in." Charlotte waved her in, almost sloshing bourbon out of the glass. Charlotte never laid the tumbler to rest while she took Cheryl's coat one handed and hung it on a coat rack in the vestibule.

Charlotte's flip-flops echoed as they walked across the white marble floors to a small library. A fire crackled merrily in the maw of a large stone hearth. Charlotte motioned her to a comfortable couch and sat beside her.

Charlotte asked, "So, what brings you out on such a horrid night? I'm afraid George isn't here. He's away on business."

Cheryl replied pleasantly, "Actually, Charlotte, I came to talk to you about groundskeeping."

Charlotte sipped her drink. "What an awful topic. I do despise all the mess it makes when they clean the grounds. And the winter is such a dreary time, don't you think? Wouldn't you rather talk about parties and get-togethers with just us girls?"

Cheryl played along. "But what about the men who do the work? Aren't they just the yummiest things out? Not that I notice such things." She made a half smile with an arched eyebrow.

Charlotte put her hand on Cheryl's. "Oh dear Lord, honey, you don't know the half of it. I always slip them a few extra dollars to do the work with their shirts off." She cackled loudly.

Charlotte took another long drink finishing the tumbler off. She inspected the empty glass. "Well, would you look at that: empty. That just won't do. Follow me to the kitchen while I get a refill—as a matter of fact, you don't seem to have anything in your hand, my dear. There's nothing worse than partying alone. I gave the staff the night off." Charlotte waved her hand around the room. "And this freaking cathedral George has put me in only makes it seem all the emptier."

She stood a little unsteadily taking Cheryl by the hand. "To the kitchen, my dear. That's where all the good stuff is. That miserly old goat puts the cheap booze in here for the guests, while he keeps the good stuff hidden away in the pantry, but I figured it out! Ha!"

Cheryl followed her. She found herself in the same narrow hall as the night of the party. The kitchen was bright and white. It was large enough to cater parties and still homey enough with an antique white enamel kitchen table with red trim. Charlotte opened a cabinet and grabbed another tumbler and a bottle of Woodford. She turned and looked at Cheryl. "Ice or neat?"

Cheryl replied, "Neat is fine. That's the way I've drunk it since college."

Charlotte filled her glass, took a long draw, and capped it off. She filled Cheryl's tumbler to two thirds and placed the bottle between them. Cheryl hoped she was not intending to finish the bottle.

Charlotte plopped back heavily in a chair at the kitchen table. "So, why in the world would you be interested in landscaping?"

Cheryl took a sip; the smooth dark bourbon burned her throat. "Not so much landscaping as landscapers, I suppose. Do you know all your workers here?"

Charlotte laughed. "I dare say I don't know any of them, nor do I care to." She put her glass down and pushed it away from her. "They're not really what I would call my kind of people." She winked at Cheryl.

Cheryl replied, "I was really interested in one of those fellows named Skeeter. I think he might be doing some illegal things on the side."

Charlotte stopped smiling. "What kind of things, my dear?"

Cheryl took another tiny sip. "Things like threatening people."

Charlotte gave her an odd look. "So why would you think I would know anything about the Skeeter person?"

Cheryl was point blank. "Well, I noticed you talking to him on the night of the party."

Charlotte nodded. "Well, isn't that the oddest coincidence. I do remember one of the hired help was here, and I believe I asked him to go get some ice."

Cheryl eyed the industrial size ice machine to Charlotte's back. She replied, "I'm sure I'm mistaken. Who could imagine a man like that in a place like this?"

Cheryl felt someone at her back. She turned in time to see Skeeter grab her neck and arm and force her to the table sloshing the Woodford out of the tumbler.

Skeeter leaned close to her. He stank of body odor and cigarettes. "So, Dr. Blumenthal, just what kind of man do you *think* I am?"

Cheryl fought against the rising tide of panic. "The kind that pulls the wings off butterflies for fun."

Skeeter paused for a moment. "I think I'm offended by that. I happen to like butterflies."

Cheryl looked at him with one eye. "It's hard to tell from this angle."

Skeeter looked at Charlotte. "She's a feisty one, Lotty. Can I have some fun first?"

Charlotte leaned back and took another drink. "Sure, just save some of that energy for me later, ya hear?"

Skeeter chuckled. "You know I always got something for you, girlie."

Charlotte looked evilly at Cheryl. "Let her up, Skeet."

Skeeter twisted her arm behind her. His grip was powerful, the arm lock hurt.

Charlotte looked at Skeeter. Her voice took a different tone. "Make sure to spread her over the South field. That way she evens up the fertilizer on the lot. It will balance out against our poor friend, Lester. God rest his soul."

The back door crashed open, and armed men in FBI vests rushed in, weapons drawn. "FBI, don't move!"

A large burly agent grabbed Skeeter away from Cheryl and pushed him face down on the table. Skeeter mumbled, "Didn't hurt."

Another agent asked Charlotte to stand. "Charlotte Wise, you are under arrest for conspiracy to commit murder. You have the right to remain silent…"

But evidently not the good sense. Charlotte screamed and pointed at Skeeter. "Why are you arresting me? It was that man over there who killed all those people in Georgia!"

Skeeter screamed, "Shut up, you stupid cow!"

Now cuffed, he began to struggle toward Charlotte. Cheryl backed away. The burly agent grabbed Skeeter's hair and slammed his head onto the table again, this time almost breaking his nose. Blood smeared on the white enamel.

Skeeter muttered, "Didn't hurt."

Cheryl backed into Dwight. She looked over her shoulder, startled. He placed a comforting hand on her shoulder. For the first time she saw him smile. Their eyes met. "You did good, kid. We got it all on the recording."

Cheryl managed a weak grin back. "Good. This crap is beginning to itch." She reached under her blouse and removed the wire taped to her bosom.

They both laughed. Charlotte and Skeeter both shot them a dirty look.

Cheryl's phone rang. She looked at the number and swallowed hard before she answered. "Hello, George. We need to talk."

The voice on the other end responded, "Yes, Cheryl, we do. Come to my office first thing in the morning."

Chapter 17

The morning rain pattered against the windowpane. She smoothed out her suit in the mirror. She took a deep breath and looked at herself; her reflection looked plastic. She closed her eyes and thought of Amit. When she opened her eyes, her smile was warm and genuine. The uncertainty of the meeting with George had her stomach in knots. He was a powerful man. It would be simple for him to ruin her reputation and future. But this was not about her. It was about the hospital and people she believed in. The people at Wise Regional needed a champion. They needed someone looking after them that cared. They needed her. She had taken an oath to heal the sick. She could not do that if she was not there.

Amit was behind her. Gently he pulled her to him. He whispered in her ear, "You are the most courageous person I know. I believe in you."

She turned. She looked into his deep brown eyes. "I don't feel courageous. I feel scared."

He replied, "And yet, you move forward. In the face of uncertainty, you don't hesitate to do what is right. That is the definition of courageous. You will be fine. Trust me."

She kissed him lightly on the lips. Softly she said, "I trust you. Now unhand me before you wrinkle my suit."

Smiling, he twirled her and let go.

She looked at him. Her gaze fixed on him, deadly serious. "I need you to know. This is not about me. It's about protecting the people at Wise Regional. I will not rest until we have fixed this. I'll tell George that, and if he's going to fire me, that's fine. I'll work until he runs me out with the law. I don't care."

Amit regarded her somberly. "There was a doctor who was held by the Nazis in a concentration camp. His name was Viktor Frankl. He survived the concentration camp. He said something along the lines of '*Those who have a "why" to live, can bear with almost any "how."* ' You have your 'why.' Now figure out the 'how.' "

Cheryl suddenly knew how she was going to do this.

****

George's secretary let her in his office. She didn't wait. "George, I know you're angry with me and you're probably going to fire me, but I need you to know I believe in Wise Regional and I'm willing to do anything to save it. If you'll give me a chance!"

George held up his hand. "Cheryl, sit."

She stopped and sat on the edge of her chair. She opened her mouth, but he put his hand up again.

George began, "Cheryl. I know you probably think I'm furious about all this. And I probably should be, but I'm *not*. There are two things I need you to understand. One—I realize you were acting in the best interest of the people at the hospital. I've spoken to Ray. He has explained to me in detail that you have turned the morale of that institution around in a very short period, and it shows. Considering yours and Ray's history, that means a lot coming from him. Things are working better. The patients are more confident, and the intake has increased because of that confidence. I built that hospital because I believed in making a difference in my community. I started my career by delivering newspapers downtown. It's an antiquated idea, but then, I am a bit of an antique. And two—you have saved me from a personal disaster with my wife. Charlotte has always been a bit flighty. That's why I love her. But after talking to Dwight at great length last night, I learned she has done a lot of bad things behind my back that damaged the reputation of the hospital and me personally. So what we are going to discuss this morning is not about your termination, but about how we are going to manage public relations around this mess."

His eyes narrowed. "I have my own issues to deal with. I suppose I'm partly to blame for this. Charlotte was impatient. I gave her everything she wanted but a large lump sum of money. She couldn't wait. So she convinced my idiot son to orchestrate this mess, so she could leverage a real estate deal through a dummy corporation. It was quite clever, though, like many things Charlotte did, she didn't think things through. For right now, we need to focus on the hospital. I need you to be the strong leader that you are and turn public opinion in our favor. Once the news media gets hold of this, they will run it into the ground along with the reputation of a lot of fine people. Are we clear?"

Cheryl narrowed her eyes. "Crystal clear. Who do we have available that can help us with the press?"

He sat back and took a draw on his cigar. "I have a firm on retainer. They work out of New York for the most part, but they're sending a man this way. He is a public relations specialist named Peter Rankin. He is flying into Greensboro and will drive here. He is your new best friend."

Cheryl nodded. "Understood."

George regarded Cheryl. "Now that all that drama is past us, on a personal note, I think you should know, you just saved me a bundle of money."

Cheryl felt puzzled. "How so?"

His eyes sparkled mischievously. "You just gave me a free pass on the divorce. There's no judge in the state that would rule in favor of a philandering homicidal maniac in divorce court. Of course, all the embezzled money is going to cost me. We're not sure how deep the rabbit hole goes. My idiot son is up to his neck in the mess. I'll have a separate conversation with him over this."

It would take some time to get all this sorted out, and in the meantime she had a hospital to save. There was sincerity in Cheryl's reply. "George, thank you for believing in me. You could have easily stopped me at any time and buried this. You had faith in me. I am committed to the people of the hospital and what it stands for."

To George's surprise, she suddenly stood, walked around the desk, and plucked the cigar from his fingers. He raised an eyebrow and started to protest. She raised her index finger silencing his protest. "And when did I say you could start smoking again?"

He tried to protest, "But—"

"No 'buts,' George. Leave this alone. The only time I want to see you in the ER is to do a walk-through tour. If you're coming to see me, it needs to be through the front door. Are we clear?"

He gave her a glum look. "Yes, Doctor."

With that she leaned over and hugged him. "And despite what the public opinion says, I think you're a good man."

****

At nine thirty a.m., Peter Rankin arrived in the front lobby. Marge called Cheryl's office and when she answered, Marge spoke cryptically. "Dr. B, there's a man here. He's tall, dark suit, sounds like he's from out of town."

Cheryl stifled a laugh. "So, Marge, does this tall, dark-suited man have a name?"

There was a pause on the other end of the line. "Rankin, Peter Rankin. With Phillips and Associates."

Cheryl replied, "I'll be down to pick him up in a minute, Marge. Thank you."

Marge responded, "Yes, ma'am. I'll hold him here."

Cheryl chuckled, "You do that, Marge."

Peter was a polished man with an erect stature and an expensive suit. He had a Hollywood row of capped white teeth. When Cheryl was close enough, he extended his hand. "Hello, Dr. Blumenthal. Peter Rankin, with Phillips and Associates. It's a pleasure to meet you."

She returned his smile. "It's Cheryl, and it is my pleasure as well."

He carried a black Italian portfolio in one hand as he walked with her to the office. He settled into the chair across from her desk. "Our senior partner, Jacob Phillips, extends his personal assurance that Phillips and Associates is here to serve you in every step of the way as consultants on this communications journey."

Cheryl tried not to sound condescending in her response. "That is most gracious of you. Yes, we could certainly use some of your expert advice on this."

Peter grinned. "Cheryl, we don't offer advice; we offer solutions to your public interface needs."

Cheryl realized Peter was a true professional. The statement was almost patronizing but so veiled she was not offended. He was a politician through and through. "So, how do we get started, Peter?"

Peter opened his portfolio and pulled out two identical agendas. One he placed before her, the other he held. "I work best with a well-structured plan. We will begin with your background story in full detail. Once we have established the key focal points of the narrative, we will shape the method of delivery to the press. Then, I will personally coach you on delivery and prep you on potential questions that could take you off track."

She blinked at the agenda. It would take days to do all of this. She had a hospital to run. She asked Peter, "Is all this necessary? It's a small town. I would be willing to bet today's lunch that just about everybody in town knows what happened."

Peter shook his head. "Cheryl, that's why you retained Phillips and Associates. What people have is their version of what they *think* happened. What we need to do is shape their vision so that they see it from our point of view. We can't allow people to form their own opinions, that's dangerous. We need to help them see this from a more diverse perspective."

Cheryl sighed and thought to herself, *This is going to be a long three days.*

****

Cheryl drafted no less than four different scripts. She was working on the final touches while Peter called the television and local papers to determine interest and timing. This was turning into a media circus. He had reached out to television stations as far away as Charlotte to carry the story. She mined through all the edits and notes from her script. When she read it aloud, it sounded like a complete fairy tale.

"To improve efficiency and effectiveness of patient care platforms at the Wise Regional Hospital, the staff has undertaken a deep exploration into solution-based patient care. Staff and doctors have streamlined diagnosis processes and sought the most rigorous methodologies available in the medical field today…"

Huh?

Cheryl looked up at Peter. "What has any of this got to do with George's wife embezzling money from the hospital?"

Peter made a sly narrow smile. "Everything and nothing. People want to be reassured that everything is under control and that their welfare is being considered and improved. That's what you're giving them."

Cheryl raised an eyebrow. "I thought this was about telling the truth."

The sly smile never faded. "The truth has many forms. This is the one that will help them see the positives—that is what they want. Positives."

"When is the press conference?"

"Tomorrow at two p.m. That gives us the rest of this evening to work on delivery and your poise during questioning. If you open a door for them, they will waltz right in and tear you to shreds."

Cheryl raised both eyebrows this time. *From politically correct to barracuda in five seconds. That must be a best in class record in his world.*

Peter had yet one more trick up his sleeve. He pulled out a video recorder to capture her practice.

For the first time since this had begun, Cheryl felt fear. Real fear. She had survived being fired, she had survived attempts on her life. She had even survived an FBI sting operation where she was used as human bait. But now, he was going to record her reading a statement as a practice run. This sent chills down her spine.

She practiced reading the statement on film for three hours. Each time he pointed out where her hands were, how she inflected her speech on certain words. She was horrified at how many times she said "Um" during the rehearsal.

At four o'clock they stopped. Peter looked at Cheryl. "You've done a phenomenal job today, Cheryl. We need to work on your attire for tomorrow. What will you be wearing?"

Cheryl was mentally weary from the continued practice sessions. "A gray suit, I guess."

Peter shook his head. "No, I think we need to update your appearance a bit." He stepped out of her office and re-entered with a box from a shop on Fifth Avenue. "I took the liberty of guessing your size. I hope you don't mind. I put you in a size twelve."

Cheryl looked dumbfounded. This man was scary. "Yes. That's perfect."

She opened the box to find a stunning black suit with gilt-edged mother of pearl buttons and a subtle gold trim on the collar and lapel. The silk blouse had just a hint of a vee lace complementing the jacket. It looked like she might have something nice to wear to the next dinner party she went to, assuming she was ever invited anywhere again after this.

Peter broke her moment. "Do you like the suit?"

Cheryl never took her eyes off it. "Yes. Good heavens, yes."

His never-ending smile continued. "So go home tonight, get a good night's rest, and I'll meet you back here at ten."

Amit met her at the apartment when she arrived home. Max circled her leg lovingly as Amit kissed her. She fell back on the couch and covered her face. "What have I gotten myself into?"

He sat beside her. "At least we still have jobs."

Cheryl replied, "Jobs?"

He regarded her coolly. "Of course. Do you think they would keep me if you were fired?"

She made a face. She hadn't even considered the consequences to Amit if she failed. "I am so sorry. I dragged you into all this. If it weren't for me, you would be relaxing with Bambi or whatever her name was, living a peaceful life."

Amit replied, "Her name was Belinda, and I chose my path. I chose substance over frivolity. I do not regret my choice."

Cheryl kissed him and rested her head on his chest. Of all the men in the world, she had chosen the right one.

Chapter 18

Cheryl entered the lobby to find it a beehive of activity. A team of men positioned chairs around a podium in the corner. Spotlights were being erected and positioned so that the lighting was centered on the podium. Peter spoke to men with sound equipment. Marge watched over the circus with utter fascination. Her chin rested on the palms of her hands.

Cheryl walked over to Marge. "Any messages, Marge?"

Marge blinked as if she had been awakened from a spell. "No, ma'am."

Cheryl looked over the procession. "I'll be in my office."

Before she could walk away, Peter spied her and motioned in her direction. "Cheryl, what would you say your signature color is?"

She snorted. "The smock of the day."

He blinked. The joke went over his head. "I'm sorry—what?"

She changed to a more direct tangent. "Blue."

Peter replied. "Yes. I can see that. The suit looks smashing on you. I have some people coming in who will manage your hair."

Cheryl gave him a quizzical look. "My hair?"

He nodded. "Yes. You have a wonderful head of hair. We just need to update your style a bit. Pony tails do not play well in this arena."

Cheryl took a deep breath. "I see. Let me know when and where I need to be. I'll be in my office."

Peter turned his attention back to the sound man. "No, no, no. We must have the speakers directed toward…"

Cheryl escaped to her office. The memos and decisions were piled up. Ray appeared in her door. "Hi, Cheryl. Is this a good time?"

She peered at him over the mound of paperwork. "As good as any. How can I help you?"

He began slowly. "It's about Delores."

Cheryl sat back. "What about her?"

"She is sitting in her office like nothing has happened. What do we do with her?"

Cheryl thought for a moment. "However unwitting she is, she's been implicated in this. We can't very well leave her in her position or with the hospital for that matter."

"I agree. Do we need the board to convene and make a ruling?"

Cheryl thought on that for a moment. "I don't think we have the luxury of that. Put her on administrative leave until we can convene with the board. We'll classify this as exigent circumstances. While the FBI is still analyzing this, she could potentially destroy evidence. That would be bad. What is she doing?"

Ray grimaced. "Painting her toenails."

Cheryl sighed. "Bring her to me. We'll do this together."

Ray nodded and left. Cheryl closed her office door and called FBI agent Luke Davis. The receptionist rang her through to Luke's office. "FBI Agent Luke Davis.

How may I help you?"

"Hi, Luke. It's Cheryl Blumenthal."

Agent Davis replied, "Cheryl, how are you doing? Is there anything wrong?"

Cheryl responded, "Fine. Thanks. No, I have a question. We're preparing to put Delores Smythe on administrative leave because of the implications of her involvement with the embezzlement. I need to put an acting financial officer back in her position to handle daily matters. Do you have any concerns with our accounting supervisor, Daniel Case?"

Agent Davis responded, "His name hasn't come up. Let me run a background check on him before we give you an answer."

Cheryl replied, "Fair enough. How long will it take?"

Agent Davis responded, "Not long. We should know in twenty-four hours."

Cheryl replied, "Thanks. We're suspending Delores this morning."

Agent Davis responded, "That's appropriate. She is a part of the investigation; she could compromise information."

There was a knock on the door. "She's here. I've got to go."

Agent Davis replied, "I'll call you back."

Cheryl hung up and walked to her door. Delores stood with Ray. She looked confused. The toe separators for painting her nails were still in place on her bare feet.

Delores spoke, "Ray said we had a meeting this morning. I didn't remember a meeting. I'm sorry."

Cheryl replied, "Come in, Delores. Have a seat."

Delores sat. "Will this take long? I have a hair appointment at ten."

Cheryl blinked. She had never met anyone this detached from reality. "No, it won't take long. Delores, the hospital is under investigation currently. Because your actions are being investigated, we need to place you on administrative leave until we can determine what our next actions will be."

Delores blinked. "What does *that* mean?"

Cheryl took a deep breath. "It means that you can go to your hair appointment and stay at home until we call you."

Delores tried to form a thought. "So I don't need to come into work?"

Cheryl replied, "Yes. That's what I mean."

The thought formed. "Oh, so I can stay at home. Will you pay me?"

Cheryl looked at Ray, who nodded. "While we review our current position, yes."

Delores grinned. "So, it's like a vacation?"

Cheryl spoke very carefully. "It's administrative leave with pay for three days. At the end of three days, we'll review this again. Okay?"

Delores replied, "Okay. Don told me this would be an easy job."

Cheryl narrowed her eyes. "You mean Don Reagan?"

Delores responded, "Um hum. He's my boyfriend."

Cheryl processed the statement for a moment before responding. "Okay. We're finished now."

Delores stood. "Thank you for the vacation."

Cheryl tried to remain composed. "We'll call you."

Ray walked Delores back to her office to gather her

things and then to the front lobby. Marge eyed her suspiciously. When she was out of earshot, she asked Ray, "What's up with her?"

Ray looked at Marge. "She's on a special assignment."

Marge looked up at Ray. "What a load of bologna."

Ray sighed and walked away.

At twelve thirty, the hairdressers and makeup artists arrived at Cheryl's office. Raul worked on her hair while Alphonso did makeup. They chattered at each other like a married couple. In precisely one hour, Cheryl looked at herself in the mirror. She was stunned. She looked like a news anchor. Her blonde hair gently draped over her shoulder; the makeup was flawless with a hint of color on her lips and eyes. She normally didn't care about hair and makeup. Maybe it was time.

Peter appeared at her door. "Perfect. Raul, Alphonso, you have done it again. Her inner radiance has shone through!"

Cheryl suddenly felt as though she were a puppet on a string. It was not a good feeling. She looked up at Peter. "Do we need to go downstairs and wait?"

Peter shook his head. "Oh no, my dear. We wait until the last moment. We don't want to make them wait, but at the same time, we can't give them time to form opinions on you either. We arrive at exactly the right moment. That is the way it is done."

Cheryl stared at the clock. Then the press statement she would read. Her anxiety grew.

Peter could sense it. "Let's get your vocal cords limbered up."

The exercise was nonsensical. She followed his example through what seemed like a ridiculous mantra.

"We ooo we ooo we ooo. Pbbbbbttt. Ooo we ooo we ooo we. Tuck tuck tuck tuck."

She was sure there was a hidden camera somewhere.

They arrived at the podium at precisely two p.m. There were only a handful of people and one television camera from a local television station. The crowd was calm, which she took as a good sign. Peter sat in the front row smiling. She began as instructed, "Good afternoon. I have a prepared statement after which I will take questions. To improve efficiency and effectiveness of patient care platforms at the Wise Regional Hospital…"

She finished the statement without a flaw. "Are there any questions?"

One hand rose. "Ed Caldwell, Center Point Gazette. What's going to happen to the hospital now, Dr. Blumenthal?"

Cheryl had been prepped for this question. "Thank you for your question, Mr. Caldwell. It is the consensus of the board of directors that the hospital will continually improve the accountability of its assets in order to deliver premium service at an affordable cost to consumers." She saw the confused look in Ed's eye.

What she said next was unscripted. "Honestly, Ed, this hospital was in some pretty serious trouble. But we've got good people who want to make a difference. That goes all the way up the chain. I spoke to George, and he's going to make this right. I loved working as an ER doctor here, and as the director, I'm committed to making this the best hospital for the people in this town. I don't want you to have to worry about sending your family thirty minutes across the county to another hospital. We are committed to making Wise Regional your first choice, not your last resort."

Ed scribbled notes on his pad. "Thank you, Cheryl. My mom's doing better thanks to you."

Cheryl replied, "Keep her away from starchy foods, and bring her back to see me for a checkup in three months."

The man from the Charlotte paper stood up and walked out without uttering a word. The camera crew wrapped up and began to put away their equipment.

Peter Rankin's smile faded for the first time in three days. All his carefully prepared work had faded into a conversation between two people.

Cheryl looked over at Marge at the desk smiling at her. She stepped off the small podium and walked over. "What are you smiling about?"

Marge winked. "They tried to make you something you weren't, and it didn't work. You're the real deal, Dr. B."

Cheryl looked at her quizzically. "I don't follow."

Marge elaborated, "That fellow from New York tried to turn you into a politician. You're too good for that. You showed them you are a real person that cares. That's what everybody loves about you, Dr. B."

Cheryl replied, "Thank you, Marge. I'm sure I won't get a Christmas card from Mr. Rankin. But people need to see we have heart, not just a great management system."

Peter Rankin walked up behind her. "Well, Cheryl, that went—well, I suppose."

Cheryl grinned. "It went better than I expected. Thank you, Peter."

Peter looked puzzled. "I am a bit surprised that the

turnout was so low."

Marge chimed in. "I can help with that."

Peter raised an eyebrow at the perky receptionist. Drolly, he asked, "Please, enlighten me?"

Marge eyed him unimpressed with his keen fashion sense. "There was a bad wreck on Interstate 77. All the real crews are covering that. Let's face it, if it bleeds it leads."

Peter replied, "You have a point." He extended his hand to Cheryl. "Cheryl, it has been a wonderful experience working with you. Even if your delivery was a bit unorthodox, you did a masterful job. Please call me if you need any further assistance. George has us on retainer."

*****

Cheryl arrived early the next morning. The lobby was cleared of all traces of the press conference the previous day.

Marge handed her the morning paper. The headlines of the Center Point Gazette read *Community Stands Behind New Director of Wise Regional*. "Like I said, Dr. B. You're a real person who cares. People can't fake things like that."

Cheryl looked curiously at Marge as she handed her an envelope. "What's this?"

Marge replied impatiently, "Well, open it and see."

Cheryl wasted no time in ripping it open.

You are cordially invited to a piano recital featuring young artist Dalton Hope performing Chopin's "Raindrop" Prelude. April 5th at 2 p.m.

Cheryl came around the desk, Marge stood, and they held each other close. Tears streamed down their cheeks. Cheryl finally managed to choke out, "Oh

Marge, how wonderful!"

Marge wiped her cheek. "I know, isn't it? If you hadn't stood firm, he would have never played again. We have saved you a place on the first row. The pastor at the Methodist church is going to let us play there."

Cheryl wiped away her tears. "I will be there no matter what."

Chapter 19

Weeks passed since the press conference. Life at the hospital fell into a routine. Cheryl walked the floor daily checking with her supervisors and doctors. People seemed genuinely happy to see her coming. Horace continued to work part time in the Childcare Center. In the meantime, a qualified staff member, Marcie Malone, had been hired to run the center. She was young, energetic, and likeable. Horace gave Cheryl the thumbs up on her.

As Cheryl did her daily walkthrough, little Melody ran to her. "Dr. B, Dr. B, come see my picture!" She took Cheryl's hand and walked her to the table where a picture of a stick figure with a stethoscope had a large yellow sun and what looked like a dog or cat.

Cheryl picked up the drawing and said, "That's wonderful, Melody. Is the doctor helping the dog?"

Melody beamed, "Oh yes. This doctor helps everything! The dogs and cats and people and flowers."

Cheryl smiled. "That must be some doctor."

Melody was excited. "It is! That's me! I'm going to grow up and be like you!"

Cheryl hugged her. "Melody, you're going to grow up and be an amazing doctor."

Melody went back to coloring her drawing.

By eleven a.m., Cheryl was in her office poring over reports. The phone rang.

"Cheryl, this is Dwight Ironsides."

Cheryl replied, "Hi, Dwight. Is everything okay?"

Dwight responded, "Yes. I have some news for you. The agency has finished with the investigation. Charlotte Wise has been indicted on conspiracy to commit fraud and conspiracy to commit murder; her son and two other former staff members have taken pleas. Don Reagan was caught up in the whole mess as well. And our friend Skeeter has been indicted on murder charges. It seems that Lester was a victim of Skeeter's lawncare business."

Cheryl responded, "I'm afraid I don't follow."

Dwight was a little more straightforward. "It appears that Skeeter murdered him and ran him through the wood shredder."

Cheryl gasped. "Oh no!"

Dwight elaborated. "It appears as though that was the plan for you. If they couldn't get you to play along with the scheme, you would have been next."

A chill went down Cheryl's spine. She remembered the statement Charlotte made about spreading her over the south field. She shuddered involuntarily. "Please tell me he's safely behind bars still."

Dwight chuckled. "I doubt if he will ever see the light of day again. If they can convict on the conspiracy charge on Charlotte, she'll most likely get twenty-five to life."

Cheryl asked the burning question, "Will I have to testify in court?"

Dwight replied, "Not likely at this point. They have enough physical evidence. I doubt it will go to a jury trial. Most likely they'll take a plea over the death penalty."

Cheryl asked, "What about the money? What happened to it?"

Dwight responded, "That's pretty interesting. They bribed some state official to tell them where the ramp was going to be off the interstate, and the money was used to buy real estate. They were working on a deal to sell the land to a super retail center and a chain gas station which would have tripled their return. There is still an ongoing investigation on how the bank lent the money. It appears that some of the bank executives worked in collusion to embezzle the money and received kickbacks. Every time we turn a corner, there's another layer to analyze. You really uncovered a hornet's nest on this one. Any regrets?"

Cheryl replied thoughtfully, "No. Every one of them took advantage of the system and almost left this institution in shambles. They were greedy. It's sad, but they got what they deserved."

Dwight was silent for a moment. "I couldn't agree more."

They hung up. As soon as the phone hung up, it rang again. Louise was on the other end of the line this time. "Cheryl, you need to come down to the ER, now!"

Now what could it be?

She rushed to the ER. Her mind raced. There was something in Louise's voice that was different. Something she hadn't heard before. A knot formed in the pit of her stomach. She cleared the nurse's station to be met by Boomer and Louise. The look in their eyes told the story; she just wasn't sure she wanted to know. Cheryl furrowed her brows. "Who is it?"

Louise and Boomer looked at each other. It was Boomer who spoke. "We have a Morgan Blumenthal in Room 7. We've started a drip. I don't know how much time he has."

Cheryl looked stunned. "My dad?"

Louise took her by the arm. "Honey, I know this is a shock. He asked for you directly. There's a woman in there with him."

Cheryl had not seen her father since the night he left them. The emotions ran wild. Was it possible? She shrugged off Louise and almost ran to Room 7. She ripped the curtain back and saw him lying in the bed. A tanned, tattooed dirty blonde in a torn "Legalize Weed" shirt stared at her. There was fear in her eyes. Her father's eyes were open. Without looking at her directly, Cheryl addressed the blonde, "Leave us." The woman practically vaulted from the chair.

Cheryl held her emotions in check. "Hello, Father."

Her father replied, "Cher, it's good to see you, honey."

She didn't respond. Instead, she looked at his chart. The EKG looked bad. He was on borrowed time. "Dad, your heart is failing. We're going to give you some drugs to see if we can stabilize you. We might be able to get you on a VAD unit and repair some of the damage."

Her father responded, "Cher, I know we don't have much time. I came to make things right between us."

Cheryl stared at him. "How, Dad? How can you possibly make things right? You abandoned us. Mom died a little bit each day after you left. She worked two jobs until the day she died. I got a job as soon as I was old enough to work and did nothing but study and work to get through medical school. I tried to tell myself that it wasn't me. But how could I know that? And you show up now? Why didn't you just crawl back in the hole you ran into and take the blonde bimbo with you?" Her hands were trembling so bad the chart fell from her hands onto the floor.

Her father took a deep breath and closed his eyes. "Cher, what I did was wrong. There is no excuse for it. Every day with your mother was torture. She blamed me for everything that was wrong with her life. Every day she reminded me I was a loser and that's all I would ever be. That last night was the last straw. I was standing in line at the store. I had a loaf of bread and a pack of cigarettes. When I got to the counter, I had enough for one thing. I chose the cigarettes. It was at that moment I realized your mother was right. I *was* a loser. I figured you would be better off without me. I'm dying, Cher. I can't undo the past. I can't make you love me. All I can do is tell you that I never stopped loving you. I swear—"

His eyes rolled back into his head. The monitor screamed out the flatline tones.

Cheryl reacted immediately. "Boomer! Bag him! Louise, get the AED over here!" Cheryl began to do chest compressions. She felt his ribs crack under the strain. She kept pumping.

Louise called out, "Clear!" The AED shocked him. His body jumped. He was still a flatline.

"Clear!" The machine hit him again. No response. His face began to turn blue. The team threw everything they had at him.

It was Boomer who called it. "Cheryl. I'm declaring."

She sat back and stared at him. Louise cleared away the bag mask and pulled the sheet up to his chin. She placed a hand on her shoulder. "Honey, I'll give you a minute. I'll go let the girlfriend know."

Cheryl looked up at her. "No. This is something I need to do."

Louise gave her a concerned look. "Are you sure about this?"

Cheryl nodded. "I'm sure. It's the right thing to do."

She walked out to the lobby. The blonde looked up. Tears welled up in her eyes. Cheryl walked up to her and wrapped her arms around her. None of this was her fault.

"I'm sorry. We did everything we could do." She could feel the woman sobbing in her arms. Her mascara smeared on Cheryl's tan blazer.

The woman looked at her. "He really did love you. He was afraid to see you—he knew you would be angry with him. It would have been closer for us to go to County hospital, but he insisted we come here. I don't know what I'll do without him." She began sobbing again.

Cheryl realized there were tears streaming down her cheeks as well. They cried together in the waiting room. Louise's strong arms guided them to the chapel.

****

The room smelled of carnations and furniture polish. Mr. Brice was a short portly man with a thinning comb-over and empathetic brown eyes behind horn-rimmed glasses. "Ms. Parrish, what did you have in mind for a budget on the services?"

Doris and Cheryl sat across the desk from him.

Doris rolled a tissue in her hand. "I, uh, I really hadn't thought of it. Can I make payments?"

Cheryl watched her fumble for a moment more. She wasn't a bad woman. Cheryl had learned about her father's history with Doris, and she had no part in his leaving. It was unfair to put her in this position. She placed a hand on Doris's and looked at Mr. Brice. "Let's plan on something economical and respectful. Cremation and a small service here in the chapel. I'll take responsibility for the cost."

Doris looked relieved.

Mr. Brice looked at Cheryl. "Thank you, Dr. Blumenthal. When would you like to plan to have the service?"

Cheryl responded, "Let's plan for Thursday evening. Does that sound all right, Doris?"

Doris replied, "I called his uncle. He's letting the family know." She blew her nose. It was evident to Cheryl that this was taking its toll on her.

****

On Thursday evening, the family arrived in one car. It was a faded Oldsmobile with no hubcaps. Cheryl could not recall a single person in the car. Her great uncle Mal and aunt Faye were an odd pair. He was a large rude man and his wife Faye was a petite, almost bird-like woman. There were two cousins she did not know.

Mal's first words were "When's the dinner start?"

Cheryl studied him carefully for a moment before responding. "This is a simple service. We did not plan for a wake."

Mal mumbled under his breath, "What a waste." He then proceeded into the chapel.

Horace, Amit, Louse, and Boomer arrived in Boomer's Benz. This was probably the most depressing funeral Cheryl had ever seen.

Mal cleaned his fingernails with a penknife while the preacher delivered a generic eulogy. Immediately after the service, Mal made a meager attempt to be respectful and said, "Sorry for your loss" without looking up. He then loaded up the group in the Oldsmobile and left.

After the service, Doris placed her hand on Cheryl's arm. "I have something for you, if you'll take it."

Cheryl followed Doris to her Cruzer with peeling flame decals. Doris reached into the dash and removed a worn brown envelope. She handed it to Cheryl who opened the envelope not knowing what to expect. In it were pictures and clippings of Cheryl through the years. He had been at her high school graduation. There was a picture of her receiving her diploma, and another of her at her college graduation. She wasn't sure how he slipped in, but there it was. There were recent articles in the local newspapers all the way up to the Gazette feature story about the community standing behind her at the hospital. He had meticulously followed her every move. Doris looked at Cheryl with tears in her eyes. "I know he failed you as a father. I know you can't forgive him for that, but please consider that he never stopped loving you. He just couldn't bring himself to face you until the end."

Cheryl took Doris's hands. "I know this was not your fight. It's obvious that you loved my dad. I'm over being angry with him. I was shocked to see him after all these years. But I'm not a scared twelve-year-old girl anymore. This closes a chapter in my life. I never knew why he left, and a part of me always wondered if it was because of me. It's clear to me now that none of this was because of me. I was just one part of a much bigger equation. I'm at peace with it, really—I am."

Doris looked relieved. "That means a lot to me, ma'am. And I know your daddy would have been pleased to hear that too."

Cheryl hugged Doris. "I wish you well, Doris."

Doris managed a smile. "You too, Cheryl." Without ceremony, Doris got in the aging Cruzer and left.

She felt a presence behind her. Amit's arms pulled her close to him. His familiar voice sounded in her ear. "Boomer has offered to take us to dinner at the Copper Kettle. Are you up for it?"

She nodded. "I am. And since I have a designated driver, I might take the night off for a change."

They walked hand in hand to Boomer's car.

Chapter 20

It was a gorgeous morning in early spring. The azaleas and dogwoods were in full bloom. The excited chitter of birds in the early morning air raised a symphony of sight and sound as cardinals swooped and darted in the fragrance of a Carolina morning. Cheryl snuggled deeper under the covers. But this was not a day to lie in bed. This was the day of the recital; she would finally hear Dalton play. She picked out a pale yellow floral print for the occasion with white flats with a pink bow. Cheryl pushed her bangs back as she looked in the mirror. She'd kept her hairstyle from Raul so her blonde hair lay perfectly on her shoulders covering the spaghetti straps completely.

Amit had gone in early today but promised to meet her there on time. It was a perfect day. Max circled her legs in the kitchen looking for a morning treat and cuddle. She opened windows in the apartment to let in the fragrance of the morning air. She carried a cup of coffee to the balcony; the small enclosure was big enough for a small table and two chairs. It overlooked the playground of pines and azaleas which acted as an arena of aerial acrobatics. Max watched as well, though his focus was not so much on the amazing skills of the birds but more along the lines of a tasty brunch.

Cheryl watched Max as his tail twitched and he tribbled at a robin on a loblolly pine branch nearby. She looked at her watch and decided she had enough time to get a manicure before the recital. She grabbed her purse and headed to Ms. Wong's Nail Emporium in the strip mall down the street.

At Ms. Wong's, Susie was her manicurist. The big red chair was comfortable but did nothing to mask the smell of acetone in the salon. Susie looked up at Cheryl. "You want me to do your eyebrows? Only five dollars."

Cheryl smiled. "Just a manicure."

Susie pushed. "You want me to do your feet? I'll smooth them out, real nice."

Cheryl remained firm. "Just a manicure. Thanks."

Susie buffed her nails. "You know. Sandal season is next month."

Cheryl looked at her seriously. "Just a manicure."

Susie filed her nails deftly. "You going to a special event?"

Cheryl sighed. "Yes. A piano recital."

Susie replied, "I fix your eyebrows, real cheap."

Cheryl caved. "That sounds nice. Do my eyebrows."

Susie persisted. "Me do your feet?"

Cheryl was firm. "No. I don't have time for a pedicure. Just a manicure and eyebrows. Okay?"

Susie grinned up at her. "Okay. If that's what you want."

When her nails were buffed, polished, and filed, Susie used the ancient torture technique of waxing the eyebrows. The wax felt nice going on. A little warm, of course. Then when it had cooled, Susie told the lie she had told a thousand times, "This won't hurt a bit."

Cheryl blinked back the tears after Susie ripped the few hairs from her eyebrows away. She vowed to never get waxed again. Ever. But she had to admit, she was smooth.

She arrived at the recital at 1:45. She was surprised at the number of cars in the parking lot. She assumed that Dalton must be performing with other students and their parents were there as well.

As she entered the church, a young usher named Randall walked her to a seat in the front row. She was amazed at how many people she knew in the sanctuary. She waved and smiled at most of the people she walked past. It looked like everyone from the hospital had shown up. It warmed her heart to see so much support for Dalton. At the same time, she wondered who was at the hospital. She sat beside Marge and James on the front row. She noticed they were holding hands. She suspected they had become close. This clinched it for her.

Dalton's piano teacher introduced several young performers. Cheryl was enthralled that such small children could play so well. The audience entertained meaningful renditions of "Chopsticks" and "Mary Had a Little Lamb" while everyone waited for Dalton's solo.

Amit slid in beside Cheryl. He was handsome in his white silk shirt and black slacks. The black closed-toe Italian sandals reminded her of how much he hated regular shoes. He whispered, "Sorry, I got caught up."

She placed her hand on his and squeezed. Dalton entered the stage. She watched fascinated as Dalton began to embrace the keyboard. It was a Dalton she had never seen before. The strains of Chopin's "Raindrop" filled the room. Dalton was at one with the keys. His body moved with the rhythm of melody. Tears began to stream down Cheryl's cheeks as she watched him perform. The memory of Granny Ruth and the old Philco flooded forth. Not a sound could be heard beyond that of the baby grand piano. She reached over and took Marge's hand. Marge looked at her, tears welling in her eyes.

Dalton finished the piece, and there was a stunned silence across the room. He stood, turned, and faced the audience. As he bowed, an eruption of cheers and applause filled the church. People rose to their feet. Calls of "Bravo!" filled the room, followed by calls for "Encore!"

Dalton grinned and raised his hand. As the cheers and applause subsided, he spoke. "Before I go on, I have a request." He extended his hand toward Cheryl. "Dr. Blumenthal, would you join me on the stage?" Surprised, Cheryl stood. Carefully, she worked her way toward the stage. Dalton reached behind the piano and lifted a bouquet of yellow roses. As she approached, he extended the flowers toward her. "Dr. B, if you hadn't done what you did, I would not be able to perform today. Thank you for being who you are."

Cheryl was humbled that she had a small part in this, wiped the tears from her eyes. And took the roses from his hands and leaned over to hug him tight. She started to leave, but he stopped her. "Wait." He resumed his place at the piano and began to play Debussy's "Clair de Lune."

Amidst the softness of the melody and the stillness of the moment on stage, Cheryl did not notice Amit had walked up behind her. Gently, Amit placed his hand on her shoulder. She turned toward him, as he lowered himself to one knee. Her eyes widened. Dalton continued to play softly in the background. He smiled as he looked up at her. "Cheryl Blumenthal, will you be my wife?" He held the ring toward her. Her hand was shaking as he eased a one-carat filigree marquise diamond onto her finger. She placed the flowers on the piano and wrapped her arms around him. "*Yes! Yes! A thousand times yes!*"

The next chorus of cheers and applause almost drowned out Dalton's "Clair de Lune."

Though she would later deny it, it was said that Louise shed a tear of her own as she yelled at the top of her lungs, "Thank you Lord Almighty, *yes!*"

Epilogue

Seven years later, Dalton Hope entered Juilliard by way of George Wise. He is a promising young talent in the school.

Margery Hope tied the knot with James Kennedy. Dalton now has two little sisters, Melody, who is an aspiring artist, and a new addition to the family, Emily, who is quite the handful, as it turns out.

Luke Davis was promoted to senior forensics analyst with the FBI for his work with finding where the money was hidden when it was embezzled from Wise Regional Hospital. The ten million dollars was recovered and paid back, clearing all debts for the hospital. Since then, Wise Regional has become so successful at patient care, it has expanded three times. It has now surpassed County General in patient intake and satisfaction.

Cheryl and Amit have three children who are frequent visitors at the Horace Peebles residence. Barley the dog is quite happy with the visits and playing fetch with Ruth, their youngest daughter. Barley is especially happy when Ruth has ice cream and it is his mission to ensure her small face is clean of any residue.

George Wise continues to smoke cigars in private against doctor's orders but has entered a new relationship with a lady he met in Spain two years ago.

He continues to woo her, but she has not said "yes" so far…

Dr. Blumenthal, now Dr. Patel, has implemented a benchmark program at Wise Regional where medical students seeking residency are screened to participate in a program at the hospital targeting low-income families with free preventative examinations and discounted treatment for hypertension and diabetes. The program has been so successful that it has a waiting list of students to enter the program.

And Horace Peebles decided to share the final poem from his grandmother's book with Cheryl, which was dedicated to Horace's grandfather. So, I thought I might share it with you…

In the Darkness the Knight Came

And lo in the darkness of my day, my knight arrived,
His hands were hardened by the fertile soil,
His heart was sweetened by the endless toil,
He asked me not for my adoration,
He asked me thus for my self-contentment,
His well of kindness touched my heart,
His bottomless depth captured my soul.
And lo my Knight rescued me,
From my plight on Whisper Park Lane.

A word from the author...

Before my late sister took her life, she told me we are late bloomers. I waited five decades to put pen to paper in earnest, and I now appreciate her counsel. In the autumn of life, I have untethered any reservations and allowed my imagination to roam free. My creative engine and my autodidactic methods serve me, as they have my whole life, to create memorable stories with characters you can relate to. Allow me to share my joy with you.

www.ingramcontent.com/pod-product-compliance
Lightning Source LLC
Chambersburg PA
CBHW071007280626
47160CB00015B/1617